The Pirate Curse

Also by E.J. Stevens

Spirit Guide Series

She Smells the Dead
Spirit Storm
Legend of Witchtrot Road
Brush with Death

Ivy Granger Series

Shadow Sight
Blood and Mistletoe
Ghost Light
Club Nexus
Burning Bright (2014)

Hunters' Guild Series

Hunting in Bruges (2014)

The Pirate Curse

A Spirit Guide Novel

E.J. Stevens

Published by Sacred Oaks Press
Sacred Oaks, 221 Sacred Oaks Lane, Wells, Maine 04090

First Printing (trade paperback edition), October 2012

Copyright © E.J. Stevens 2013
All rights reserved

Stevens, E.J.
The Pirate Curse / E.J. Stevens

ISBN 978-0-9842475-7-8 (trade pbk.)

Printed in the United States of America

PUBLISHER'S NOTE
This is a work of fiction. Names, characters, places, and incidents either are the product of the author's imagination or are used fictitiously, and any resemblance to actual persons, living or dead, business establishments, events, or locales is entirely coincidental.

The scanning, uploading and distribution of this book via the Internet or via any other means without the permission of the publisher is illegal and punishable by law. Please purchase only authorized electronic editions, and do not participate in or encourage electronic piracy of copyrighted materials. Your support of the author's rights is appreciated.

Chapter 1

I flinched as a shadow danced across the rocks. A seagull swooped down low, taunting me with its cries, and I froze. What would the creature do to protect its nest? I'd seen what Hitchcock thought birds were capable of, and I wasn't eager to find out if real life was as terrifying as fiction. In my life, reality was usually way scarier.

"Don't worry bird," I muttered. "I'm not here to steal eggs from your nest."

No, I had other treasure in mind. I was searching for the bones of Black Sam Bellamy, Prince of Pirates. Too bad the bird wasn't convinced.

I ducked my head against the bird's aggressive flight maneuvers and pushed myself into action, resuming my struggle to scale the mass of green and gray stone that loomed before me. Cold saltwater tugged at my skirt, threatening with the crash of every wave to tear my grasp from the seaweed-slick rocks and pull me down into the churning depths.

I dug fingernails, painted with chipped, black polish, into a narrow crevice and tried not to think about what might be lurking there. The razor-sharp barnacles were bad enough. I was already bleeding from my first encounter with the evil crustaceans. If I started worrying about what else lurked in the tide pools and rock crevices, it wouldn't be long before my imagination took over and I'd likely see dorsal fins cut through the surface of nearby waves.

I shook my head, wet hair slapping against my face. No, I wouldn't succumb to panic. There'd be plenty of time later to worry about sharks, jellyfish, and flying monkeys. For now, I had to focus on getting out of this water before the ocean swallowed me whole.

I wedged a bare foot into the space between two stones and, with a grunt, pulled myself up onto a pile of rocks. I sat dripping water and gasping for air like a fish flung onto shore.

I grabbed and twisted my skirt with both hands, wringing water onto the rocks, and surveyed the area where I sat. I was surrounded by tide pools that hovered just above the waves, at the base of a tall cliff.

Of course, that would change soon enough. These rocks would be well beneath the ocean waters once the tide came in. It was no wonder that no one had discovered the pirate's remains before now. Only a madman or a fool would come out here in search of treasure.

So what did that make me?

*****

A few days earlier...

"Come on, Yuki," Emma said. "Say you'll come with us. Gordy has his family's beach house for the entire week. It'll be fun."

Right. Fun. A week of sun and sand; I'm pretty sure I was allergic to both.

"I don't know," I said. "I have a lot of work to do here. My art stall is supposed to be open by August."

I picked at the drying paint beneath my fingernails. I did want to spend time with my friends. Emma, Gordy, and Katie would be leaving soon for college, but why did it have to be a week at the beach. Couldn't they all just stay in town and do a scary movie marathon?

"Please?" Emma asked. "Simon and I will help you guys get this place ready for your grand opening. And you can paint ghosts at the beach."

She batted her eyelashes at me and I sighed. My friend had already won and she knew it; I was just delaying the inevitable. Of course I'd go to the beach house. I wiped a drying paintbrush with a rag and stuffed it into an old pickle jar with more force than was necessary.

"Fine, I'll go, but I have a favor to ask," I said.

I swallowed hard and lifted my head to meet Emma's gaze.

"Of course I'll do it," she said.

"Wait, I haven't even said what it is yet," I said.

I frowned at Emma's serious expression. There was no way she could know what favor I was going to ask. I was the one with the bizarre psychic powers, not my friend. Not that my ability to smell the dead helped me to read minds or anything. That would actually be a useful talent.

"You want me to go with you to Salem so you can return the amulet, right?" she asked.

My jaw dropped and it took me a minute before I could speak.

"H-h-how did you know?" I asked.

"Girl, we've been friends for how long?" she asked. "I know all your secret hiding places and I've seen what you've been painting when no one else is looking."

I bit my lip and looked away. Leave it to Emma to snoop. I knew she was just worried about me, especially since she'd be leaving soon for college. It was true that I was still dealing with the PTSD fallout from my abduction at the sweaty hands of Wakefield High's football team, but the images in those paintings had nothing to do with being stuffed in a school supply closet like a dirty mop.

The paintings Emma had found were my way of coping with a different set of images that haunted my dreams. Ever since we'd stolen the amulet that helped to protect me against the spirits of the dead, I'd had nightmares about the retribution we'd receive at the hands of the amulet's rightful owners, a coven of witches.

Each night when I fell asleep, I was tormented by the knowledge that I'd put my friends in danger. When I woke, I tried to gain control over the dreams by painting the scenes from my nighttime terrors. I tried to make sense of the recurring dreams by looking for clues in the paintings, but the nightmare images were just as terrifying by the light of day. Every one of those paintings had something in common—they were filled with rivers of blood.

"You suck," I said. My voice squeaked like a mouse and I cleared my throat. "Those paintings were private."

Emma shrugged. The petite blond was tougher than she looked and stubborn when it came to helping others. She'd probably been nosing through my shop for weeks, looking for any clues that would explain the dark circles under my eyes.

"Are you really that worried the witches will come for us?" she asked.

"Yes, I am," I said with a sigh. There was no point keeping the fact I was still having the nightmares a secret. Emma would figure it out eventually. "It's the same dream every night. The witches come demanding the amulet, but before taking it they kill every one of my friends. I'm worried that the dreams are going to come true. I don't know how to explain it, but I'm sure that they're searching for the amulet and that eventually they'll find it. And I'm scared of what they'll do to us when they do."

I'd told Emma the truth. My dreams were always the same. The witches would come for the amulet and their revenge, but instead of punishing me, they hurt my friends. The guilt was eating me up inside. I had to return the amulet to the little occult shop in Salem.

"Then count me in," she said.

Emma reached out her fist and we bumped knuckles. I let out the breath I'd been holding and laughed. Maybe everything would be okay after all. I could put up with a week at the beach if it meant time with my friends and the promise of a future trip to Salem to return the amulet to its rightful owners.

I should have known it wouldn't be that simple.

Chapter 2

I gave the painting a critical eye and nodded. I'd been working on this piece for over a week, but it was finally done. The gold hued shapes made a pleasant contrast as they hovered around the small girl dressed all in black. I already had a few people interested in the painting. What those potential buyers didn't know was that this piece was a self-portrait—and the golden spirits surrounding me were real.

I first saw the gray and golden auras of spirits when I'd obtained Nera's amulet to survive Samhain. Since then, after a car accident that resulted in a head injury, I'd been gifted with the ability to see these auras without the use of the magic amulet. But, except for sharing this new development with my closest friends, I kept that information to myself. Being mysterious was good for selling art; seeing dead people not so much.

I carried the large canvas to the back of the workspace and leaned it against the wall with the others. I wiped an arm across my brow and smiled. I'd been working hard to get my art stall ready for business, and the hard work was paying off.

I couldn't have done it without Cal. My boyfriend, and local werewolf pack alpha, believed in me, and my artistic vision. Cal had put a down payment on the rental space as a graduation present. With his help, I'd have this place ready to open by mid-August. I surveyed the black walls of the small market space and grinned.

I may not be going to college in the fall, but that didn't mean I didn't have ambition. I was turning my ability to see ghosts into something positive. Using my artistic talent to express my unique world view was both exciting and terrifying, but I was up to the challenge. I was going to wow this town with art like they'd never seen before.

Hands slipped over my eyes, blocking my sight, and I squealed.

"Guess who?" he asked.

Cal's werewolf abilities let him move silently, giving him super ninja stealth, but our spirit tattoos linked us together. A familiar tingling sensation spread up my ankle and I leaned back into the arms of my assailant.

"I know that's you, Calvin Miller," I said.

The blindfold of his hands fell away and I turned in the circle of his arms.

"I didn't expect you back until tonight," I said.

Not that I was complaining or anything. Having Cal here in this moment was exactly what I wanted, like a wish granted from a fairy godmother. Though that was silly; ghosts and werewolves exist, but vampires and fairies were pure fiction.

"I couldn't stay away," he said. "I missed you, Princess."

"I missed you too," I said.

Cal, and the rest of the werewolf pack, had spent the past two days at Wolf Camp, deep in the Maine woods. As pack alpha, it was Cal's duty to be there, but Wolf Camp was also the safest place for him to be during the full moon—safest for him and everyone else. He may have been learning how to control his wolf spirit, but if Cal felt threatened during the days surrounding the full moon, things could go from bad to worse in a blur of shifting bones, fangs, and fur.

That was exactly why his being here was unexpected; the full moon was last night. Cal shouldn't have been back in town until tonight at the earliest. Not that I was complaining. I could score some extra Cal time and pass long the invite to the beach house.

If everything went according to Emma's plan, we'd all be driving up the coast tomorrow for a week at the seashore. I may not be crazy about sun, surf, and sand, but I had to admit that a week with my boyfriend and our best friends had some major fun potential. Bonus points if we had a bonfire on the beach and told scary stories.

"Yuki?" Cal asked.

"Huh?" I asked. "Oh, sorry."

I blushed and ducked my head. I'd been staring off into space, already dreaming up a good ghost story. I hoped I hadn't looked like too much of an idiot. If there was drool, I would die.

"I was saying that I can't stay long," he said. "I have to get back to Wolf Camp before dark."

"Wait, you're leaving?" I asked. "You just got here. And Emma's inviting everyone to the beach house. Gordy's uncle is letting us use the place for an entire week. I…I thought we could ride up together."

"Sorry," he said. "Simon and I have pack business to finish u, but you should go. We'll be up in a couple of days."

"Seriously?" I asked. I groaned.

"You'll have fun," he said. "Just don't forget your sunscreen, and your umbrella."

"It's a parasol," I muttered. "Fine, I'll ride up with Emma. Are you sure you'll be able to join us in a few days?"

"I'm sure," he said.

"And this thing at Wolf Camp, it's not dangerous, is it?" I asked. "Because I could come with you and lend a hand."

"I'll be fine," he said. "One of our younger pack members had her first change last night and I want to be there to answer any questions she may have. It's not dangerous, and Simon's with her now explaining how we control our wolf spirit, but I'm Alpha. It's my responsibility to teach our ways and help make the transition easier."

"Oh, okay," I said. "At least it wasn't a secret for her, like it was for you. That had to help scale down the fear factor."

Before Cal became pack alpha, young werewolves usually weren't told what they were until after their first change. The whole werewolf thing was kept a secret. But Cal said that shapeshifting without knowing what was happening to you was terrifying. He didn't want any more kids going through that. Educating adolescent werewolves about the change had been one of Cal's initiatives to help his younger pack members.

Cal's arms tightened around me and I tilted my head to study his face. His wolf spirit paced there, just below the surface, and Cal's eyes looked haunted. He knew all too well how bad things could get for a new werewolf without any training.

"I hope so," he said. Cal winced and looked away. "I want to make the first few days of being a werewolf easier for this kid."

"You'll do great," I said. I nodded and pulled Cal closer, giving him a light squeeze. "She's lucky to have an alpha like you. And I wish we could spend time together, but I get it, pack business and everything. Plus, you know, with all the emotions she's feeling the kid could probably use some Gandhi quotes about now."

Cal loved philosophy and his brain was a limitless repository of quotes from his favorite deep thinkers. It was one of the things I loved about him, though I tended more toward quoting Star Wars, Death Note, and Fullmetal Alchemist.

Cal matched my smile with one of his own and I blushed. His eyes were so blue they seemed to glow like sapphires lit from within. My breath caught and I wondered for the millionth time how I'd ever made the mistake of thinking we were just friends.

"I wish I could go with you to the beach house, but it's important that Simon and I stay at Wolf Camp until things are settled," he said. "We'll finish up, and then I'm all yours."

"All mine?" I asked. "I like the sound of that."

I pressed closer to Cal, enjoying the tingle of electricity that rushed along my skin. Our bodies and souls longed to be closer, but I hesitated. We avoided touching so near the full moon, but I was already in his arms. Would it be so wrong to hazard a kiss? I bit my lip and searched Cal's face for answers.

Cal's control was good, but was it that good? He had the whole zen-master-samurai-poet-monk thing going on, but keeping his wolf spirit under wraps took more than an iron will. Maintaining control took concentration; who could hold onto that level of focus when joining lips and skin?

My heart started to race and I decided to risk just one kiss. Cal was going away for a few days, after all, and I'd make it a quick kiss, really. Also, the zen-master-samurai-poet-monk thing? That was undeniably hot.

I slid my hands up Cal's chest, feeling the hard muscles tighten beneath the thin cotton of his shirt. His pupils widened, swimming in a deep blue sea. I fisted my hands around Cal's shirt collar and pulled him down toward me as I raised myself up on tiptoes.

Cal hesitated for a second, but surrendered to my waiting lips without much of a fight. The real battle was between him and his wolf. Heightened emotions can bring on the change for many werewolves, especially so close to the full moon.

I felt dizzy as a wave of heat poured off Cal's skin, a sure sign that his wolf spirit was close. The heady combination of heat and Cal's kisses sent a shiver up and down my spine. His arms tightened around me, the muscles beneath my hands going rigid as our kiss deepened. I could stay here like this forever, but Cal's wolf spirit was pacing too close to the surface.

With a mental sigh, I started to slow my kiss, preparing to pull away. Cal began to withdraw then nipped playfully at my lip, making me gasp. He swallowed my breath and his kisses deepened. My knees felt weak and I hung suspended by his encircling arms and the strength of his kiss.

Cal was always the one to put the brakes on our make-out sessions when they got too intense. But Cal wasn't pulling away. Still holding me upright with a palm against my back, Cal slid the fingers of his other hand into the tumble of my hair. He pulled my face closer and I felt the press of his incisor against my lip.

Wait. Cal's teeth didn't feel like that, not even pressed this closely together. I ran my tongue along the tip of his tooth and flinched, drawing my tongue away. That was no ordinary human tooth. Cal's incisors were lengthening into fangs.

Son of a dung beetle, how could I be so epically stupid?

My breath quickened, and this time it had nothing to do with yummy kisses. Cal and I were both in big trouble. I closed my eyes and took a calming breath, which was hard to do. Cal's fingers moved in circles against my back, making me want to melt against him. But right now I had to gather my strength and concentrate.

I tried doing math equations in my head and pushed thoughts of kissing away. To my surprise, it worked. Math is my worst subject, and the effort it took to solve equations helped to clear my head. I blinked up at Cal, but his eyes were closed. I didn't want to make any sudden movements. I wasn't sure what would happen if I quickly pulled away, so instead I reached up behind my head to where Cal's fingers were tangled in my hair.

I extricated his fingers from my hair one by one and slid my hand into his. Cal's fingers immediately entwined with my own, releasing my head from his iron grasp. Tiny dots of pain pricked the back of my hand and I knew without looking that Cal's nails had elongated into claws. I continued my mental math equations and tried to calm my racing heart.

My stomach fluttered as I pressed my other hand against Cal's chest and slowly drew my lips away. He started to draw closer, to fill the emerging gap between us, but I pressed firmly against his chest.

"Stop," I whispered.

Cal's eyes flew open and he froze in place. He blinked rapidly and his eyes went from glazed over to brimming with tears. Cal's tanned face turned ashen and he swallowed hard.

"It's okay," I said. "I mean, you know, it was awesome, but we need to stop."

The arm at my back slid away, falling to hang at his side, and I lowered my heels slowly to the ground. I squeezed the hand that was still in mine and held his gaze.

"I-I-I'm so sorry," he said.

"Shhh..." I said, reaching up to press two fingers against his lips. He flinched, but didn't pull away. "Don't be sorry. I'm the one who stupidly kissed you the day after the full moon. I, um, shouldn't have done that."

Cal tilted his head down and his hair fell into a curtain, hiding his eyes. I lifted my fingers away from his lips and tucked a lock of shaggy hair behind his ear. He was staring at the ground, a haunted look in his eyes. I lifted his chin, forcing him to meet my gaze.

"I love you Calvin Miller and you are not responsible for every foolish thing I do," I said. I shook my head and smiled. "Plus, that was an amazing kiss."

Cal let out the breath he'd been holding and reached up to run a trembling hand through his hair. When he caught sight of the claws that tipped his fingers, he froze.

"God, Yuki," he said, voice shaking. "I could have hurt you."

"Yeah, but you didn't," I said. I punched him playfully on the shoulder and grinned. "And it was a good kiss, right? I mean, maybe not worth almost going furry for, but you have to admit that was pretty awesome."

Cal let out a shaky laugh and shook his head.

"You're crazy," he said.

"Totally insane," I said, grinning like a maniac.

"Are you sure you're okay?" he asked.

Cal's brow wrinkled and his eyes roved over my body from head to toe. He pressed the palm of his hand to his heart, and I noticed that his claws had retracted. The danger was over, for now.

I inexpertly waggled my eyebrows and shrugged.

"I'm fine, but now I really can't wait for you to come see me at the beach house," I said. "After that kiss, I'm going to be counting the seconds. So you better hurry your Mr. Miyagi routine with the new kid. We have unfinished business."

Chapter 3

*A*fter helping me put away my things at the art stall, and making a phone call to check on things back at camp, Cal gave me a ride home in his truck. I babbled about the beach house and the work I still needed to finish before the grand opening of the art stall, but Cal was silent, only nodding occasionally as he clutched the steering wheel with both hands. I knew he was beating himself up over his momentary loss of control, so I made every effort to let him know that I was fine. No harm, no foul.

Our goodbye kiss was chaste for once. The worry of how close Cal had come to fully losing control of his wolf during our last kiss was a memory too close to the surface. Cal walked me to my door and with a quick peck on the cheek was gone.

I let myself into the house, and was surprised when the sounds of cooking came from the kitchen. My parents worked long hours and were rarely home. I smiled at the surprise and rounded the corner into the kitchen.

The smile fell from my face as I took in the tableau in my kitchen. The happy scene of domestic bliss I'd expected was being played out, but by the wrong actor and actress. The two people cooking dinner, while standing a little too close to each other, weren't my parents—it was Emma and Simon.

I sighed and dropped my messenger bag on the floor with a thump and walked toward the coffee maker. I grabbed a mug from the overhead cupboard and sighed.

"What are you two doing here?" I asked.

"What's the matter, love?" Simon asked. "Thought you'd be hungry after you're earlier exploits."

Emma winced and swatted Simon on the arm.

"Sorry, Yuki," she said. "Simon sensed something was wrong through the pack bond and was heading here when Cal called and said he was on his way back to camp early. Since Simon was already here, and had arranged for another wolf to stay with the new kid in his absence, Cal told him to take the evening off. He also, um, told us what happened and mentioned you might like some company."

Great, it sounded like Cal had spilled the beans about our kissing drama. I suppose with Simon sensing things through their bond, he probably guessed some of what'd happened anyway. Simon's bond wasn't quite as strong as the one Cal and I shared, but he was Cal's lieutenant after all. I snuck a glance at Simon and blushed.

Simon winked and went back to chopping vegetables. He was in my mother's apron, and I really wanted to growl at him for borrowing something that belonged to my mom—the rare times she wore that apron were precious to me—but raging at Simon was useless. And Cal was right; I didn't feel like being alone. Though, if I had a choice, Simon was about the last person I'd pick to hang out with tonight.

I walked over to see what Simon was cooking and relaxed. At least he wasn't preparing meat. I was a vegetarian and not in the mood for a food debate with a carnivorous werewolf. Maybe Emma's veganism was wearing off on him.

I grabbed a slice of sweet pepper from the cutting board and crunched on it as I grabbed milk for my coffee. I was suddenly ravenous.

"So what are we having for dinner?" I asked.

Emma smiled and strode to the counter, waving her arms to encompass a pile of vegetables, a bowl of black beans, and a stack of flour tortillas.

"We're making your favorite," she said. "Veggie burritos."

"They'd be better with steak," Simon muttered.

"What was that?" I asked.

"Nothing," he said.

I smiled behind my coffee mug. Maybe Simon wasn't so reformed with his eating habits after all.

"Gordy said you and I are welcome to drive up to the beach house tonight, you know, after Simon heads back to camp," Emma said. "I guess Katie's making a big breakfast tomorrow morning, and the waves are supposed to be awesome."

"I don't surf," I said.

"But you do eat," she said. "And it might be fun to watch. You could even try painting the surfers out on the water."

I shrugged and set my mug in the sink.

"I guess I could go pack," I said. "How long until dinner's ready?"

"Long enough," Simon said. He loped up behind Emma and put an arm around her waist. "Take your time."

I rolled my eyes and headed for my room. I paused on the stairs and looked back to see Emma swat Simon with a towel. He ducked and stole a kiss along her neck, eliciting a squeal and a smile from Emma. He turned back to the cooking with a swagger and I shook my head.

I just hoped they were more careful than I had been with Cal. It was still less than twenty-four hours since the full moon after all. Simon had more control over his wolf spirit than any other werewolf, but everyone has limits.

I turned away from the happy scene and took the stairs to my bedroom two at a time. I was glad my friends were here and that Emma and Simon had become such a great couple, with none of the cheating behavior I'd worried Simon would bring to the relationship, but I was glad for an excuse to escape.

I grimaced and bit my lip. After what happened earlier with Cal, I didn't feel much like thinking about kissing. I clenched my fist and rushed to my room. I closed the door and leaned against it, gasping for air. I'd done something really foolish today, but I swore an oath never to do something like that again. I hadn't just put myself in danger; I'd risked my relationship with Cal. I knew with absolute certainty that if I'd pushed Cal too far and he'd hurt me, he would have ignored his feelings for me and broken things off for good.

With no ghosts haunting me, no serial killers on the loose, and Cal and Simon running the pack efficiently, I'd let my guard down. That was where I'd made my first mistake—a mistake that could have ruined everything. I should have known better. Our lives were woven through with things we didn't understand, and powers beyond our control. No matter how good things got, we had to remember one thing—there's always a storm on the horizon.

*****

Finished packing, I lugged my hatbox-shaped suitcase and overstuffed messenger bag down the stairs. I dropped both bags onto the narrow bench in the front entryway and cut through the living room to the kitchen. Emma dragged me over to the table, and Simon waved a spatula toward a plate heaped with veggie burritos. I'd had a minor meltdown up in my bedroom, but if anyone noticed the puffy, red circles around my eyes, they didn't mention it.

I checked out the spread of toppings, eyes widening. Simon and Emma had been busy while I'd packed my suitcase—and not in the way I'd worried about. The table was covered in small dishes piled high with chopped onions, diced tomatoes, shredded lettuce, and vegan cheese. There was even fresh, homemade salsa and guacamole. My stomach growled and Emma laughed.

"I told Simon that you'd be hungry," she said. "He didn't believe me."

I narrowed my eyes at Simon and hid my smile.

"You doubted Emma's wisdom?" I asked.

"I didn't doubt you'd be hungry," he said, shaking his head. "Heaven knows you eat more than a wolf after a hard winter." I scowled at Simon. I didn't eat *that* much. I just had a healthy appetite, so long as I wasn't being haunted by any smelly ghosts. "I had merely suggested ordering pizza for dinner."

"Meat lover's pizza," Emma said, frowning at Simon, hands on her hips.

"That, Love, was a joke," he said.

"Well, pizza and veggie burritos are in my top ten favorite foods, but I'm glad you went with these," I said, gesturing at my plate. "They smell amazing."

Emma and Simon joined me at the kitchen table and I dug into the stack of burritos. Emma was right, I was hungry. While I ate, Emma told us all about her plans for our week at the beach house.

"Why the big rush to get to the beach house tonight?" I asked. "Our original plan was to leave in the morning."

"Katie has a big breakfast planned," Emma said, studying her plate.

I had a feeling it was more than that.

"So, we just get up early and hit the road in time for breakfast," I said. "Unless there's another reason you want to be there tonight."

I let a weighty silence hang in the air and Simon laughed as he carried his plate to the sink.

"She's onto you, love," he said. "Might as well tell her now."

"Tell me what?" I asked.

Emma sighed and looked up from her plate.

"Atlantic puffins have been dying in large numbers and washing up on beaches up and down the coast," Emma said. "I just thought that I could try to help any living birds that wash up while we're there."

"You want me to go to a beach that's covered in dead freaking bird corpses?" I asked, chest tightening.

Emma had to be kidding. She knew I avoided dead things. I doubted I'd be haunted by a flock of ghost puffins, but I was still repulsed by the idea. Emma sighed and pinched the bridge of her nose.

"There haven't been any dead puffins on the beach where we're going, yet," she said. "But I wanted to be there, just in case. It's a slim chance one will even show up."

"But you want to rush up to the beach house tonight, just in case?" I asked.

"Yes," Emma said. "It's the fault of human beings that the fish population has been reduced so low that the poor puffins are starving. I want to be there to help."

When she pushed her shoulders back and set her jaw, I knew I'd lost the argument. I sighed and slumped in my chair.

"Might as well admit defeat, love," Simon said, tossing a dish towel over his shoulder. "There's no winning against the plight of suffering animals."

For once, Simon was right. Emma would badger me all night. If I wanted a chance of sleep tonight, I'd give up now. It looked like Emma and I were heading out to the beach house. At least there'd be a big breakfast to look forward to in the morning.

"Fine," I said. "Bring on the puffins. It can't make the beach suck any worse than it already does."

Chapter 4

Once Simon left, with a promise to join up with us in a few days, we loaded up the car and headed out to the beach house. It was a long drive since it was getting dark and Emma was worried about hitting migrating turtles, but we finally made it to the house without the need for her veterinary skills. Luckily, the beach was free of sickly puffins and we turned in early. I took that as a sign that this trip would be free from animal drama and pesky ghosts. I should have known better.

I was enjoying breakfast the next morning when the alert on Emma's phone startled me from my happy food-coma. Katie had made a huge breakfast, as promised, that included massive, fluffy waffles, vanilla bean ice cream, and fresh strawberries. I'd already eaten a stack of waffles and was happily mopping up the last of the ice cream on my plate when Emma's phone chirped.

If I had the talent, I'd have raised an eyebrow at my friend. I settled for making a questioning "hmmm?" sound around the mouthful of food.

"I know we just got here, but I have to go," Emma said.

She carried her smoothie glass to the sink and turned on the faucet full blast. When the noise stopped, I swallowed and narrowed my eyes at my friend.

"You can't be serious," I said. "Don't tell me you're leaving me here."

"Dude, it's puppies, I have to go," she said. She was perfectly serious. I twisted the paper napkin in my lap and started tearing it into little pieces. "There's a raid on a New Hampshire puppy mill in two hours. If I leave now, I can make it back by tomorrow morning, tomorrow night at the latest."

"But what about the dying puffins?" I asked.

"Most of the puffins are already dead when they wash ashore," she said. "I can do more good at the puppy mill, and if all goes well, I'll be back in time to save puffins too."

"You're really going," I said.

"It's puppies," she said, letting the words sink in.

I rolled my eyes and sighed. Of course it was puppies. Emma had dragged me here last night on the promise of an uninterrupted week together. Okay, a week of possible puffin rescue, but a week at the beach all the same. That plan hadn't involved my friend ditching me while she ran off to save the planet. But I shouldn't have been surprised. Emma was a loyal friend, but she was even more devoted to her causes. In Emma's worldview, saving puppies was right up there with world peace.

I tossed a pile of napkin confetti onto my plate and lifted my head to look Emma in the eye. I was ready to argue about the sudden abandonment, but Emma was pointing to her phone which displayed the sad faces of tiny, wiggly puppies. I shook my head and slumped in the chair, putting my elbows on the kitchen table. *Why did it have to be puppies?*

"Fine," I said. "Go save the puppies."

"You rock," she said. Emma grabbed her backpack, slung it over one shoulder, and tossed her other arm around my waist. "I'll be back as soon as we safely relocate the puppies, promise."

Emma swished out the door where she said her goodbyes to Gordy and Katie. Within seconds, I could hear the crunch of gravel as Emma's car backed out of the driveway. I glanced out the window to where Gordy and Katie had resumed their morning makeout session, which would be followed by their afternoon and evening makeout sessions.

I groaned and lowered my head into my hands. I didn't drive, and my only ride out of this place just left. My options were either to be trapped in the beach house with two lovebirds or to risk the sun, sea, and sand.

I went into the guestroom where I'd stashed my messenger bag. I tucked a parasol under the flap and slung the bag over my shoulder. On the way back through the kitchen, I grabbed another sugary waffle and shoved it in my mouth. I left a hastily scrawled note on the counter for Gordy and Katie and silently pushed open the screen door at the back of the house.

Chapter 5

I rinsed my sticky hands at the water's edge and wiped them down my skirt, wincing at the sun's blindingly bright reflection on the water. I took a step away from the ocean, and blinked away the black spots floating in my vision. Not that there was much to see. It was so sunny, the entire beach looked whitewashed.

Squinting against the sun, I dug through my bag until I turned up a pair of sunglasses. I slid them on and felt the low throb of an emerging headache settle. I crossed my fingers and prayed that the migraine was not of the supernatural kind. I hadn't smelt anything funny, yet. But if the rest of the day was anything like my morning, I didn't have high hopes.

Have I mentioned how much I detest the beach? The sandy parts are filled with loud, scantily clad tourists and, well, *sand* and the rocky areas are strewn with slippery seaweed and stink of rotting fish.

I took one look at the kids playing volleyball and the rows of bodies baking in the sun like wieners on a grill and turned toward the rocks up the coast. If I had to be at the beach, I might as well work on some sketches and I couldn't do that here in a crowd of cheering voices and scornful looks. I'd take my chances with the seaweed and rotting fish.

Of course, there was no avoiding the sun. I opened my lace parasol and trudged down the beach, my heavy boots leaving a line of prints in the sand, like a ghost following in my footsteps.

I stepped over the brightly marked safety boundary constructed of neon yellow, coarse, nylon rope and orange striped buoys, leaving the crowds and lifeguards behind. Leaving the safe swim zone was like walking into another dimension. Except for the occasional person out fishing or surfing, I had this stretch of beach to myself.

I continued walking, constantly reminded why I disliked the beach. The heat and sun were making me sweat and the sand in my boots was rubbing my ankles raw. *Why did Emma have to drag me to the freaking beach of all places?*

I wiped my forehead, scowling at the smudge of white face powder now on my black shirt sleeve, and drank from my water bottle. I'd been walking toward the rocks for half an hour, and in most of that time the small, black mounds remained in the distance, tiny dots on the horizon like a mirage. But now I stood at the outskirts of the craggy coastline, large rocks half buried in the sand at my feet as if the gods had dropped them carelessly from the sky.

I walked around the smaller outlying stones until I came to a pile of rocks and old storm debris that formed the boundary of a small cove. I lowered my parasol, tucked it into the strap of my messenger bag, and climbed onto the rocks. The pile of stone and driftwood formed an arm that reached out into the sea, holding a small body of water and a tiny patch of sandy beach in its embrace.

I lifted a hand to shield my eyes against the late morning sun and a grin lifted my lips. The long walk had paid off. I'd found the best spot on the entire beach. There wasn't another soul on the rocks or the tranquil beach below.

This place is so totally perfect.

I climbed down the other side of the rock pile, thankful that I'd worn my knee-high combat boots. The stones were tossed here precariously by the waves, without a thought for the safety of stubborn trespassers. The danger of a turned ankle increased as I lowered myself down the northern face of the stone. The rocks here were wet from the previous high tide and slick with green algae.

When I reached the bottom, I stood on a partially shaded patch of sand. The rocks looming overhead blocked the sun. Too bad they also blocked the breeze coming off the ocean. The air here was completely still—and carried with it a carrion stench.

Well, almost perfect.

I wrinkled my nose at the smell. It really did stink of dead fish and rotting seaweed. Not that the fishy odor was a deal breaker. I was used to being plagued by smelly things; it's like my superpower. After a few years of smelling ghosts, I was a pro at tuning out weird odors.

I turned my attention to finding a comfy rock. Finding a suitable rock to sit on was more difficult than I thought. Rocks aren't exactly soft or ergonomically designed, but I settled for one that wasn't too pointy. It was located in a shady patch of sand at the base of the debris pile and had been worn smooth by the sea.

I sat down and started rummaging in my bag for supplies. I twisted the water bottle into the sand and settled my sketchpad and charcoal pencils onto my lap, and scanned the beach for something interesting to draw. I dismissed the bat-shaped cloud and the rock that looked like an elephant.

Movement at the water's edge caught my attention and I smiled. A flock of tiny birds were running back and forth, seeming to taunt the lapping waves as they narrowly avoided being soaked by foamy water. I sat watching the birds' hijinks, captivated by the blur of their itty bitty legs as they ran.

Soon the air was filled with the scratching of charcoal on paper as my sketchbook came alive with drawings of the playful plovers. (I knew they were called plovers after taking note of signs I'd seen during my walk. All along the dunes, signs warned of their protected status. I figured Emma would want to check into the poor, endangered birds as soon as she got back from saving puppies. And I had to admit, they were totally cute.) When the sun climbed high into the sky, stealing my shade, I paused long enough to wedge the handle of my parasol between two rocks, propping it at an angle above me.

Later, after a lunch of Skittles and trail mix, I slipped the sketchbook into my bag and stared out at the glittering waves. Sitting here in this cove, it was easy to pretend that I was all alone on a far away planet. Perhaps the diminutive birds were the masters of this alien world, their dance with the waves the source of power that gave them the gift of flight.

My eyelids felt heavy and I leaned back, listening to the ebb and flow of those waves, and dreamed of alien worlds ruled by tiny, feathered masters.

Chapter 6

*I*t wasn't long before my dreams were invaded by zombies. Alien birds just aren't all that interesting.

These were total Romero zombies, lurching along in search of tasty brains. I avoided the shambling walk of the nearest zombie and searched for a weapon. Right on cue, a shovel materialized, but not in my hand. The potential weapon was up the street, leaning against a coal shed. This would have been awesome except for the half dozen zombies hanging out by the shed moaning "braaains, braaains" like a broken record.

This dream was giving me two options. I could attempt to run past the zombies and grab the shovel or forget arming myself and run in the opposite direction like flying monkeys were hot on my tail—flying *zombie* monkeys.

I hesitated, unsure of what to do, and that's when things got weird. Well, weirder. This dream was already up there on the bizarro scale. The zombies were surrounded by feathers, I assume from grazing on the local bird population, but there were no longer any living plovers in sight. Apparently, zombies have a mega big appetite.

After consuming all the tiny bird brains, the zombies turned to larger prey. This zombie town that had appeared on an empty alien world was suddenly filled with screaming humans. Don't ask me how. I'm guessing dream logic is pretty flimsy.

All around me zombies grabbed at the humans, trying to munch their brains. But none of the zombies came toward me, which kind of ticked me off. I mean, here I was standing in front of them with a perfectly tasty brain and nobody wanted to eat me. I glowered at the zombies and the humans. It was like high school all over again. It just didn't seem fair.

I stomped over toward the shed, ready to work out my frustrations with the shovel, but was stopped by a tap on my shoulder. A zombie was standing behind me, decaying eyebrow raised, holding a cracker topped with a dollop of brain.

"Pardon me, do you have any Grey Poupon?" he asked.

I put my hands on my hips and narrowed my eyes.

"No, I don't have any Grey Poupon," I said. "I'm fresh out of condiments, but I do have a question. What is so wrong with me? I mean, not that I really want you to or anything, but why don't you want to eat my brain?"

He opened his mouth to answer, but I never learned what the zombie was going to say. He wobbled, trying to catch his balance, as the ground at his feet churned. A huge beetle burst up through the earth, raining soil on our heads.

The zombies and the humans scattered, leaving me with a seven foot tall dung beetle.

"Why would I want to eat your brain, child?" she said.

"Um, never mind," I said. "Bad dream."

"Dreams hold knowledge, little one, they are never bad," she said.

"Okay, right, I'll keep that in mind," I said. I sighed, wondering what my dung beetle spirit guide could possibly want. "So, um, what are you doing here in my dream? Wait. Is Cal okay?"

"Do not worry, child," she said. "Your wolf is safe. This is about you."

I let out a shaky breath. Cal was safe; there was nothing to worry about.

"So, um, is this about the zombie dream," I asked. "Because honestly, I could use some dream interpretation on that one."

My dung beetle spirit guide was waving her many arms in agitation, so I clamped my mouth shut and let her speak. Not that I could avoid what she had to say. My spirit guide's words crawled around inside my head against my control.

"Listen, child," she said. "We do not have much time. Something is coming with the changing tides and it is time to open your eyes, but remember this. True love has the power to pierce the veil."

"Wait, do you mean my love for Cal?" I asked.

But that didn't make sense. Cal and I were both alive. Why would we need our love to pierce the veil between the dead and the living? A shiver ran up my spine and I hugged my arms to my chest.

"It is time, child," she said. "Open your eyes."

Chapter 7

I felt Emma's cat lapping at my hand and tried to push Chairman Meow away. But something was wrong. My hand pushed impotently against cold water. There was no cat, and I wasn't sleeping over at Emma's house.

I was at the beach.

I jumped, heart racing, now fully awake. Opening my eyes only added to my panic; the beach seemed unnaturally dark and gloomy. I blinked, trying to clear the shroud of darkness, but it didn't go away. I turned my head to see the sun setting below the cliffs behind me. How long had I been asleep?

Cold water hit my fingers again and I gasped, bolting upright. I scrambled to pull myself further onto the rock, away from the water. My bag, which had been resting on my lap, slid down toward the reaching waves, but I caught it by the strap before it sank out of sight. I grabbed the messenger bag and clutched it to my chest, but my water bottle was gone—along with the sandy beach.

The tide was steadily creeping in all around me, and the setting sun cast long shadows across the rocks that were all that was left of the beach. The white sand had disappeared, swallowed by the shifting sea.

With shaking hands, I strapped my bag across my back and shoulder and jammed the parasol under the strap. I inched further up the rock and surveyed my options. The rocks beside me were too steep to climb; the step-like stones I'd descended earlier in the day were already under water.

I wasn't going to make it back the way I'd come. The cliffs at my back were also impossible to climb, but the rock arm on the opposite side of the cove looked promising. If I timed it with the waves, I could run across a thin strip of gravel along the bottom of the cliff to the other side of the cove without getting too wet. Then it would be a matter of jumping and grabbing one of the brick-shaped handholds that projected from the side of the rock formation and climbing up the huge wall of stone that thrust up through the sand like the shoulders of a giant.

The line of jagged rock that looked like the giant's elongated arm formed a jetty that extended its fingers out into the ocean. The fingers, wrist, and forearm were already submerged beneath the crashing waves, but if I could make it to the top of the shoulder where it backed onto the cliff face, I should be able to stay dry while waiting out the tide.

At least, I hoped the waves wouldn't reach high enough to smash against those rocks. If they did, I'd have to take my chances with climbing the cliff face. My darting eyes took in the sheer face of stone that towered above the cove and I started to sweat despite the cooling air around me. I let out a puff of breath, like I'd been sucker punched. Who was I kidding? I'd never survive that climb.

I pressed my lips together and turned my attention to the approaching waves. It was now or never. With shaking hands, I tucked the ends of my long skirt into the top of the waistband and shifted my bag further onto my back. I'd need my hands and legs unencumbered. I stepped one foot in front of the other and leaned forward into what I hoped was a runner's stance.

I waited until the waves receded and then sprinted across the beach, boots pounding against the wet sand. I surged forward and, with an unladylike grunt, vaulted over the approaching wave. I hurdled onto a shelf-like projection of rock and reached blindly for something to hold onto. The stone beneath my fingers was cold and damp, but I held on tightly as the wave crashed less than two feet below my boots. Salt water sprayed my bare legs and I shivered.

The waves roared before once again receding, but they were gaining ground with each surge. I sucked in air and looked for hand and toe holds in the large rock formation above my head. I didn't want to move, but it was obvious that the ocean would soon overtake the place where I clung to the rocks.

Come on Yuki, you can do this.

I frowned at the rock. From a distance, it hadn't looked so large and imposing. Now that I was clinging to it like a half-drowned lemur, I could see that I had a long ways to climb.

Fortunately, the rock was riddled with rectangular projections where I could place my hands and feet. I took a deep breath, reached for the nearest handhold, and began my ascent.

By the time I made it to the top, I was soaking wet and shaking from exhaustion. I thought my arms were going to fall off. It was like the twitchy muscles you get when French braiding your hair multiplied by a thousand. I wiped my bruised hands down the front of my blouse and surveyed the rock where I stood. I needed to find a sheltered spot, preferably one that was dry.

Too bad the rocks all looked the same in the dark. It was almost impossible to tell what was wet and slippery, and I didn't relish the idea of falling to my death or sitting in a puddle. While I'd climbed, the sun had continued to set behind the cliffs, leaving the rocks buried in the gathering gloom.

I searched my bag and grinned when my hand felt the cool, metal shaft of a flashlight. After a particularly terrifying experience trapped in a dark cave with a murderous werewolf, I come more prepared than a Girl Scout. I flicked on the flashlight and shone it around the rocks at my feet.

Not everything is a big fan of light. Some creatures prefer the dark—and most of them are pretty nasty. Something scuttled to my right and I jumped. A crab scrambled toward a shadowy crevice away from the flashlight beam. I reached out a hand to steady myself and sighed. Falling because of some creepy, spider-like crab would be just my luck.

Avoiding the crab, I shuffled over to a hollow in the rock that formed an alcove facing the sea. Wincing at complaining muscles, I lowered myself into the sheltered space and pulled my skirt around my legs. It wasn't the most comfortable place to wait out the tide, but it would have to do.

I aimed the flashlight into my messenger bag and searched its contents. I'd remembered to bring my sketchbook, sunglasses, parasol, food, and water, but I'd eaten the food hours ago and the water bottle had been taken by the greedy waves. I shook my head at the sunglasses and parasol and put them back in my bag; they wouldn't do me any good in the dark.

I sighed and picked at my nails. I'd forgotten my cell phone back at the beach house, which left the sketchbook as my only means of communication. But unless a bottle washed up onto the rocks, I wasn't sending messages any time soon. I hoped that Gordy and Katie wouldn't worry when I didn't make it back in time for dinner.

I flicked off the flashlight, conserving batteries, and let my eyes adjust to the twilight. In the expanding darkness, the formerly tranquil cove grew menacing. Wind dug its fingers into my damp clothes, making me shiver, and the waves seemed to growl as they bashed angrily against the rocks below.

Chapter 8

I sat hunched on the rocks for hours waiting for the tide to change. Once the moon climbed the sky, I could see well enough to track the receding waves, but there was something about being out here alone that set my teeth on edge. My perch above the waves had seemed like the safest place to wait out the tide, but now that I was up here, I was beginning to have my doubts. *I have a bad feeling about this.*

I switched the flashlight on and held it in a white-knuckled grip. The hair along my neck and arms prickled and I could swear that I was being watched. I swung the flashlight in an arc, but it was just me and the crab. I felt like one of those old-timey lighthouse keepers, alone at the edge of the world—just me, my beam of light, and the sea.

The flashlight cut a swath through the darkness as I swung my hand in an arc, and I blinked. There was something sparkly wedged into a crevice in the rock not far from where I was sitting.

I stood, muscles complaining with the movement, and peered over the edge into the cove below. A sliver of white sand, like a close-trimmed fingernail, was beginning to reveal itself at the bottom of the cliff. I'd be able to leave this place soon, but I still had time to kill. I might as well check out the shiny thing. I could use the distraction. It's not like there was cable television up here. I was bored out of my mind, and jumping at imaginary boogey men.

I tiptoed forward, shining my flashlight along the rocks at my feet. There. I crouched down and angled the light at the glint of metal. It wasn't a shell; that was for sure. I brushed away sand and tossed a piece of tangled seaweed out of the way for a better look.

I tilted my head and turned the item around in my hands. From its shape, it looked like the kind of square buckle that Pilgrims supposedly wore on their shoes. But this one was solid metal, not the flimsy tinfoil ones you see in store displays around Thanksgiving. *What was a Pilgrim's fancy shoe buckle doing here on the rocks?*

A vice-like pressure started in my temples and a headache began to throb behind my eyes. It was then that I noticed the dead fish odor that had lingered in the cove was now replaced by an even stronger scent, and I was pretty sure this smell wasn't natural. My nose filled with the scent of rum, burning meat, salt brine, and gun powder, like the smell from the cap guns Cal and I used to play with as kids.

Goosebumps prickled my arms and a shiver raced up and down my spine like spiders made of ice. I dropped the silver buckle and spun around to see four shimmering shapes emerge from the gloom. That was no trick of the light, no weird reflection from my flashlight beam. Standing in front of me were four ghosts, and three of them were gray.

But the ghost standing closest to me wasn't entirely gray or gold in color. In fact, he didn't resemble any soul I'd seen before. His aura was like a strange mutation of the two types I'd become accustomed to seeing over the past few months. This man's spirit shone like the barest glint of the setting sun on murky waters.

I swallowed hard and stumbled backward a step. Worse than the confusion of muddied colors of the strange spirit, was the trio of Grays at his back. Gold hued ghosts, though sometimes annoying, are the good guys, but The Grays were bad news. From what I'd been able to deduce from past experience, Grays were spirits whose souls had become dark due to evil past deeds or particularly violent deaths—sometimes both. The guy in the front may be an enigma, but The Grays at his back were definitely something to avoid.

As I took a deep breath, ready to jump down off the rocks and take my chances with the crashing waves below, faces stared out of the gray mist. I gaped at the men, their features becoming more distinct with every passing second. My brain screamed "RUN," but my body had gone on strike. I stared slack-jawed and glassy-eyed as the ghosts came into focus.

Recently, I'd gone from only having the gift to smell ghosts to having the ability to see their spirit auras. Sensing spirit auras had been a big step, but I've never been able to see more than a sparkle of golden light or a gathered cloud of gray smoke. This was completely different. The scowling faces of four hard men peered out of the mist, making my stomach roil.

Being able to see ghosts? That was going to take some time to sink in. Unfortunately for me, I'd have to be a fast learner. I needed my brain to kick in and start working again, soon.

The Grays stared at me hungrily and I wondered what the chances were that they'd just mind their own business and leave me alone. *Yeah, right.* I took a step back, wondering how I could possibly make my escape. It was obvious that I'd never be able to scare them off, though the urge to yell, "boo!" nearly made me giggle. Instead, I bit my lip and studied the ghosts who now stood way too close for comfort.

These men had all the signs of a tough life, and their auras were dark as coal smoke. They were all covered in scars and wore guns and knives as comfortably as I wore my favorite hoodie. A large, black man even had a sword strapped to his belt. *A sword? Now that's something you don't see every day.*

Aside from the weapons, they weren't wearing much else. Their pants, if you could call them that, hung in tatters to the knee, exposing scarred legs and bare feet. I tried not to stare at the mangled feet that hovered just above the surface of the rocks.

What had happened to these men? It looked like someone had broken all their toes. And that wasn't even the worst part. One of the men grinned, showing missing teeth, and it wasn't pretty. In fact, I was thankful I'd had to skip dinner.

When did these men die? They obviously hadn't known the wonders of modern dentistry; that was for sure. Even suffocated by the terror squeezing my chest, I couldn't help but wonder who these guys were. And maybe more importantly, what did they want?

Ghosts always want something. It's the reason why they wander the world of the living, trapped here until they can complete the unfinished business that tethers them to this plane. I'd become pretty good at helping ghosts, but I'd never tried to assist one of The Grays—and this was an entire gray ghost posse.

I tore my eyes from the ghosts and scanned the beach below. If I jumped now, I'd probably break an ankle and get swallowed by the waves. Then I'd drown and have to come back and haunt these guys for eternity. No thanks. One encounter was more than enough.

I gasped as I caught movement from the corner of my eyes—were they coming closer?—but when I glanced up, it was only the ghost leader waving The Grays back, giving me room to breathe. The Grays looked downcast as their progress was halted by the arm of the murky gold spirit.

In my terror, I'd overlooked the man who acted as their leader. He too had become more distinct. Unlike the scary guys, this man was handsome. Heck, he was drop dead gorgeous. The other men were either bald or had greasy hair wrapped in head scarves, but this man had a full head of shiny, raven black, curly hair tied back with a black ribbon.

Drop dead gorgeous? I felt a rising giggle try to escape. Since the guy was a ghost, he'd obviously dropped dead ages ago. Oh well, it didn't keep a girl from looking.

His clothes were nicer too. He was dressed in leather breaches and a velvet-trimmed leather tunic over a white shirt with billowing lace at the wrist. A sword hung from his left hip and four pistols ran the length of a red sash that crossed his broad chest. He wore a hoop earring in one ear, which gave him a roguish look that reminded me of Simon. But this guy didn't have any facial scars like Emma's werewolf boyfriend.

I studied the face beneath the shadow of a tricorn hat and winced. This man may not have been as scarred and bedraggled as his companions, but there was a deep sadness in his blue eyes that spoke of a different kind of scars—the ones left on one's heart. I looked away, avoiding his gaze, and stared down at his feet. There were silver buckles on his shoes—just like the silver buckle I'd thought belonged to some long lost Pilgrim.

But these weren't the ghosts of Pilgrims. The world tilted as the realization struck. These were the ghosts of pirates.

Chapter 9

Thankfully, the tide soon turned and I was able to leave my temporary prison atop the stone jetty. I couldn't get off those rocks fast enough. Being leered at by ghosts was no fun. Who knew pirates would be so creepy? The romance books had it all wrong; being trapped with a bunch of roguish pirates just wasn't what it was cracked up to be. I hurried up the beach, wincing at the headache that pounded with every jolting step.

I made it safely back to the beach house, trailing a pack of ghost pirates. I hadn't been lucky enough to leave them behind in the rocky cove. Nope, they'd followed me the entire way up the beach like hungry wolves stalking their prey.

I hunched my shoulders and trudged up the porch steps. I was the only one who could see or smell the ghosts, of course, but that didn't stop me from feeling like a mother duck with her brood of ducklings in tow—heavily armed ducklings. I pulled the screen door open and held it while all four apparitions walked past to gawk at the clean, white walls and blue and white furniture.

I couldn't wait to tell Emma and Cal that I'd brought a band of ghost pirates into Gordy's house. Not that there was anything I could do about it. The ghosts weren't leaving until I helped them settle whatever unfinished business they had in this world. So it was either let them tag along while I went inside, or sleep on the beach. After hours of sitting out there on that rocky cliff, there was no way I was passing up a warm bed and a hot meal.

I heard footsteps on the stairs and looked up to see Gordy rushing down from the second floor. Katie wasn't far behind.

"Yuki!"

Gordy rushed over and wrapped me in a bear hug. When he let me go, Katie ducked in and gave me a quick squeeze.

"Are you okay?" Gordy asked. "What happened? Are you hurt?"

"I'm fine," I said with a shrug. "I just picked the wrong spot to sit and sketch. Next time I'll bring a tide chart."

"I told him you probably got lost," Katie said. She blushed looking down at the floor, then up at me. "I got turned around in the dunes the first time I came here. It took me an hour to find my way back to the main beach."

Gordy shook his head and smiled.

"I forget you guys didn't grow up here," he said. "I spent so much time here as a kid, I know it like my neighborhood back home. But from now on, I'm giving everyone tours of the beaches and the dunes."

"And a map," Katie said, smiling.

"And a tide chart," I said. I mock-punched Gordy on the arm and walked toward the kitchen. "Unless you want all your company to drown."

"No thanks," he said. "I don't want a haunted beach house."

I shook my head. *If he only knew.* I continued on into the kitchen and flicked on the overhead light. Gordy just laughed as I shuffled over to the fridge and rummaged for food. After pushing aside a package of hot dogs, I pulled out a plate of cold waffles covered in cling wrap. I held up the plate and raised my eyebrows.

"Can I have some of these?" I asked. "I kind of missed dinner, and lunch if you don't count trail mix."

"Sure, you can eat them all," Katie said nodding.

I pulled off the cling wrap, grabbed a fork, and slid into a chair at the kitchen table. As Katie and Gordy watched wide-eyed, I started packing in cold waffles like a contestant in a food eating competition. Suddenly being able to see ghosts, like as clear as a hologram, had been a shock. I needed carbs and sugar.

After shoveling in half the waffle tower, I slowed down. My hand was no longer shaking and the growling beast in my belly had subsided.

"So, um, any news from Emma or Cal?" I asked. "I left my phone up in the guest room."

"We know," Katie said, exchanging a look with Gordy. "We tried to call you when you didn't come back for dinner."

"When your phone started ringing upstairs, we figured you left it behind," Gordy said.

"Sorry," I said. I focused on eating the last of the waffles.

"Emma said that the puppies have been relocated to a clinic in New Hampshire and that she should be back by tomorrow," Katie said.

"Nothing from Cal?" I asked.

"He hasn't called our cells or the beach house," Gordy said, frowning. "Was he supposed to call? I thought we weren't expecting him until at least tomorrow."

"Oh no, it's cool," I said.

I'd worried that Cal might sense my fear through our bond and come rushing down here, but apparently he hadn't even called. I should have been relieved, but a part of me was disappointed that he hadn't noticed, which was silly. It's not like I was on the brink of death or anything. I'd just been trapped on a rock with a gang of ghost pirates. No big deal.

I slumped out of the chair and plodded over to the sink where I rinsed off my dish.

"You want anything else?" Katie asked. "I can cook up some eggs or home fries if you like."

"No thanks," I said. "I'm beat. See you guys in the morning."

I made it up to the guest room, but couldn't sleep. My skin felt tight with drying sea salt and I had sand in my boots, but I didn't feel much like getting undressed. There were four ghosts wandering the house and, even though they were currently gawking at the wonders of modern kitchen appliances, it was only a matter of time before they came up to my room. And if pirates were anything like the movies, I didn't think they'd avert their eyes just because I asked them to.

Plus, most of these guys were Grays. How had I ended up with an evil ghost entourage? I shivered and grabbed a blanket off the bed. I wrapped myself up in a gingham cocoon and waddled over to the small, white table where Emma had left her laptop.

While the laptop powered on, I thought about what I knew. I had three bad guys and one, who acted like their leader, with a golden aura tainted by some evil deed. They certainly looked and acted like pirates, but I didn't know enough about coastal history to guess who they were or what they could possibly want from me.

The smell of salt brine filled the room and I turned to where the gold and gray ghost now stood. *Speak of the devil.*

If I wanted answers, I should start with him. I could return to my Internet searching later. I held up my hand and moved toward the door.

"Stay there," I muttered. "I'll be right back."

I tiptoed down the hall to a closet where I'd seen Gordy's family stash their board games. If they were like most families, someone had probably bought a Ouija board to bring out on stormy nights. I searched the closet, running my hands along the boxes, careful not to disturb Gordy and Katie. Not that I needed to worry. Soft music and muffled laughter came from the master bedroom, which meant that my friends were both downstairs.

On the top shelf, behind a shoe box filled with card games, I found what I was looking for. I pulled the box down, closed the closet door, and crept back to the guest room where my smelly guest was examining the wonders of indoor plumbing. I shook my head and waved him toward the bed where I plunked down cross-legged and started taking the Ouija board out of the box.

The handsome ghost came to settle on the bed. He sat across from me and I was suddenly once more aware of just how good looking he was. I fidgeted with the blanket still wrapped around my shoulders and let it fall to the bed. It was way too warm in here.

With shaking hands, I set the plastic pointer in the center of the board and looked up into ocean blue eyes set into a tanned face framed by dark, unruly curls. I blushed and pulled my hands away from the Ouija board.

"Okay," I said. "I'll ask questions and you move the pointer thingy to answer."

The ghost nodded. His eyes remained sad, but his lips quirked, hinting at a grin. I rested my head in my hands and thought about what to ask. Ghosts had a tendency to become unfocused and less and less responsive the more questions you ask. I had to make these questions count.

"What is your name?" I asked. I wanted to ask, "Are you a pirate?" but figured that would be a silly question.

I watched the ghost reach out and grip the pointer with both hands. His skin was so translucent that I could see the board game through his wrist. He screwed up his face in concentration and began pushing the pointer from letter to letter.

S-A-M, pause, B-E-L-L-A-M-Y. So the ghost's name was Sam Bellamy. We were getting somewhere. I flicked my eyes to the bedroom door, but no Grays, nor my friends, had appeared.

"So, Sam, what is it I can help you with?" I said. "I'm guessing there's something you want."

The ghost, Sam, nodded and started pushing the pointer around again. His hands appeared even more transparent than before. Wielding the Ouija board pointer was using up whatever ghost mojo this guy had. He started to fade, leaving those sad eyes and the answer to my last question.

The pointer slid back and forth across the board, spelling out just one word—TREASURE.

Chapter 10

I woke with a start and let out a groan. I ached all over. I clawed my way out of the tangle of blankets and removed a pointy piece of plastic from under my shoulder blade. I'd fallen asleep on top of the Ouija board. *Way to go Yuki.*

I'd waited for Sam's ghost to reappear, hoping to ask more questions. Apparently, the ghost hadn't returned and I'd fallen asleep. I looked out the window and frowned. It was way too early to be awake. The sun wasn't even up yet.

I threw an arm over my face and tried to go back to sleep, but the events of the night before haunted me. Being able to see ghosts was just too much, especially when one of them had the saddest eyes I'd ever seen. I mulled over my conversation with Sam, wondering what I should do next, but my memory of the evening seemed so surreal. This ghost wanted me to go looking for pirate treasure? That was a new one, even for me.

I sighed, giving up on sleep, and got up and trudged over to the table holding Emma's laptop. I tapped the touchpad and it sprang to life. It was doubtful that I'd find anything about some dude who probably died hundreds of years ago, but you never know. If nothing else, I could search for old shipwrecks off the Maine coast.

I typed Sam Bellamy into Google and got over five-million matches. I gasped, but it wasn't the huge number of search results that made my jaw drop; it was the pictures of pirates in the image search. The pictures didn't look exactly like Sam—they were more like those police composite pictures they sketch based on witness testimony—but the men in these images all had long, dark, curly hair and penetrating blue eyes. I clicked on the first one and read the caption, "Samuel Bellamy."

Huh, that was weird. I didn't think we had any famous pirates here in Maine, but the name and likeness were unlikely to just be coincidence. I leaned closer to the screen and clicked on an article from National Geographic.

Vampire bats fluttered in my stomach as I read down through the article. Sam wasn't just famous, he was notorious. Sam, the ghost with the sad eyes and wry grin, was better known as Black Sam Bellamy, Prince of Pirates.

According to the Internet, Sam was a "Robin Hood of the sea." He stole from the rich and gave to the poor—his crew. His crew even called themselves "Robin Hood's Merry Men." Oh, and it was obvious why his men were merry, and completely devoted to Sam. His crew were made up of poor sailors and freed slaves, many of whom Sam freed himself.

By all accounts, Sam was a fair man who ruled his pirate fleet as a leader chosen by his crew, not as a tyrant. He was voted to the position of ship's captain and led his men to victory in their pursuit of wealth and freedom.

In many ways, the young pirate had seemed to lead a charmed life. He often seemed to be in just the right place at the right time, like when he met his lady love. He'd met a beautiful girl, Mary Hallett of Eastham, during one of his stops in Cape Cod. At that time he was a legitimate sailor, working mostly on ship salvage. Mary and Sam fell madly in love, but when the star-crossed lovers approached Mary's parents' about matrimony, they refused Sam's proposal based on his lack of wealth.

In the summer of 1715, Sam left Mary to seek his fortune. Sam set sail with his friend, Palgrave Williams, in hopes of earning enough gold to gain the approval of Mary's parents. The men sailed toward the coast of Florida where a Spanish plate fleet, cargo ships carrying treasure, was rumored to have sunk. Sam and his friend had little luck at treasure hunting and soon turned to piracy. They joined the crew of the *Mary Anne*, a pirate ship captained by an Englishman named Benjamin Hornigold.

Captain Hornigold refused to attack English ships, leading to the eventual mutiny by his crew—just in time for Sam to fill his buckled shoes. Hornigold was deposed and "Black Sam" was elected as the *Mary Anne*'s new captain. Bellamy was hugely successful as a pirate, capturing many ships and their cargo, and soon had a loyal fleet at his command.

Sam and his "Merry Men" plagued ships up and down the colonial coastline and throughout the Caribbean Sea. He captured more than fifty ships in less than two years—an amazing feat for a young man who'd set out to salvage a bit of treasure off the Florida coast in hopes of earning enough to wed the girl he'd met in Cape Cod.

In the spring of 1717 he made his greatest conquest, a three hundred ton English slave ship named the *Whydah*. The ship had finished selling its cargo and was returning to England carrying a fortune in gold. Bellamy was now a rich man.

After only two years of pirating, Sam decided it was time to return to Cape Cod and the girl he loved. He'd earned more in those few years than most men made in a lifetime. With the *Whydah* laden with gold, Sam sailed toward Cape Cod and the waiting arms of Mary Hallett.

It looked like Sam and Mary would get their fairytale ending. Too bad the pirate had been cursed.

Before leaving the Caribbean Sea, Sam and his crew boarded a merchant ship and relieved the hold of its burden. Some of the online articles claimed his crew demanded one last job before sailing home, while others say Sam just got greedy. Whatever the reason, attacking the merchant ship may have spelled his doom.

While aboard the deck of the merchant sloop, a wealthy, young man demanded he be taken back to Sam's flagship, the *Whydah*, to become part of his crew. Sam refused, knowing his fleet was disbanding and he himself was readying to retire from the pirate life.

The spoilt, young merchant threw a fit and ran to the ship rail. With his hands still tied behind his back from the earlier takeover of the ship, the man climbed over the edge and plunged into the shark infested sea. But before he jumped, it's reported by his crewmates that the man turned back, and with spittle on his lips and a wild gleam in his eye, cursed Sam to never reach the one person he loved.

The merchant was believed to have gone mad from stress and dehydration and the crews of both ships thought no more of it. Bellamy relinquished the plundered ship to its captain and the pirate fleet sailed north.

With his friend Palgrave Williams captaining the *Mary Anne* alongside him, Sam again headed toward Cape Cod, the *Whydah*'s belly bloated with treasure. As the ships neared New England, Williams diverted the *Mary Anne* to Rhode Island to visit his own family. Bellamy continued on toward the Massachusetts coast, but he never reached his one true love.

A violent nor'easter struck, buffeting Bellamy's ship with thirty foot waves and hurricane force winds. At midnight, the witching hour, the winds snapped the main mast of the *Whydah* and the storm dragged the heavily laden ship down into its watery grave.

Of the one hundred and forty five men aboard the ship, only two survived. Of Samuel Bellamy there was no sign. Over one hundred bodies washed ashore, but Sam's body was never found.

Could Sam's body have been carried up the coast to Maine? That might explain his sudden appearance at the rocky cove. I read on, enthralled by the tragic story of a young pirate and his lady love.

The night the *Whydah* sank, Mary Hallet is said to have stood lashed by the storm atop a cliff overlooking the sea. Whether she was waiting anxiously for Sam's return or cursing him was a matter of much Internet speculation. Most people believed that the scorned woman had made a deal with the devil to pull the ship into a watery grave.

I didn't believe that Mary had cursed Sam's ship, heck he'd been cursed already, but I could understand why some people believed it to be true. While Sam had spent two blessed years chasing treasure and becoming a rich man, Mary's life had unraveled like an old, tattered sweater.

When Sam and Mary first met, she was considered a great catch by the eligible men of town. Her feisty independence was overlooked (since apparently, back in the day guys didn't like their girlfriends to think for themselves) in favor of her great beauty. Many of the Internet articles remarked upon her rosy cheeks and long, blond hair. At sixteen, Mary had the entire world ahead of her—until she fell in love with Sam.

Soon after Sam left seeking his fortune, Mary discovered she was pregnant. She tried to hide the pregnancy and months later gave birth to Sam's child alone. The child died that night while Mary took shelter in a barn near the home of her aunt and uncle. The girl and dead child were discovered the following morning, causing a scandal in the small, Puritan town.

Mary, distraught and exhausted from childbirth and the loss of her child, was dragged before the town selectman. She was publicly whipped and thrown in jail for bearing a child out of wedlock. While in captivity some of Mary's rebellious spirit returned and she managed to escape, but she was soon caught and punished. Over and over again, Mary suffered shame and torture at the hands of the Puritans of Eastham until finally the townsfolk cast her out.

The people of Eastham, believing Mary to be a witch, banished the girl to nearby Wellfleet. There she built a small hut on the dunes where she kept vigil for her handsome pirate. Mary became a ghost of the beautiful girl she once was. Living alone in fear, shame, and poverty with the constant threat of captivity and torture, Mary lost more than her youthful beauty—she lost her mind.

Mary wandered the dunes and along the cliffs, waiting for Sam and talking to ghosts. Her strange behavior only fueled the rumors put forth by her spiteful neighbors. They spat the words "witch" and "devil worshiper" and called her "Goody" Hallett the Witch of Wellfleet. When she was seen gazing out to sea during the storm that claimed the *Whydah*, the people of Eastham claimed that the Witch of Wellfleet had created the storm to avenge Sam for leaving her.

I clenched my jaw and felt my hand tighten around the edges of Emma's laptop. I turned away from the Internet search and took a deep breath. The people of Eastham were a bunch of bullies, even worse than the J-team.

I'd spent four years of high school tormented by bullies who taunted me by calling me a "witch." I'd been confined in a school supply closet when those same bullies kidnapped me out of ignorance and superstition. But I'd only had to endure that captivity for a matter of minutes. What would it have been like to suffer months in an 18th century prison?

I blinked away tears and crawled into bed. I fisted the covers in my hands and buried my face into the pillow in time to muffle choked sobs.

I fell back into a fitful sleep, dreaming of the Wakefield football team dressed like Pilgrims, waving pitchforks, and screaming "burn the witch!" It would have been comical if I hadn't been the one tied to the stake. And I wasn't alone. Chained to a post not far from where I'd been trussed was a blond girl with sad eyes, eyes that reminded me of a handsome pirate who never made it home to the girl he loved.

Chapter 11

I lifted my head and moaned. Sun was shining through my window, making my head throb. My eyes darted around the room, but the ghost pirates were nowhere to be seen. I sniffed the air and threw back the covers.

The Grays smelled like rum, burning meat, and gunpowder, and Sam had a scent like salt brine cologne. I didn't smell any of the above, which meant the ghosts hadn't returned. I took advantage of the brief reprieve and went in to stand under the shower. My hair was stiff with sand and salt.

After the shower, I slathered on sunscreen and dressed in a black elliptical skirt covered in silver buckled straps and trailing red ribbons, a Skelanimals tee featuring Pen the penguin, black and red striped tights, and black, butt-stomping, combat boots.

I stared at the bathroom mirror and gave my reflection a quick nod. My eyes were still bloodshot from my little breakdown last night, this morning, whatever, but I was ready to move ahead and help these ghosts find peace.

After what had happened in the Wakefield High School supply closet, I'd sworn to stand up to bullies. Mary and Sam may not have lived for a very long time, but Sam was here now and I was going to do what I did best. I was going to help a ghost with his unfinished business, and if that meant avenging his true love's torment at the hands of some Puritan bullies, all the better.

Plus, Sam had mentioned treasure. That had to be fun right? What could be more exciting than searching for pirate treasure?

Unfortunately, Sam didn't reappear. Without the location of his treasure, there wasn't much I could do. I paced the beach house, waiting for the pirates, Emma, and Cal. Katie was down by the water, watching Gordy surf, but I'd already had enough of the ocean. Instead of joining them, I opened cupboards and rummaged through the fridge looking for food. I might as well make everyone breakfast.

I was just filling the last two slots of the toast rack when Gordy and Katie came through the back door. They were giggling quietly and trying to open the squeaky door without waking the dead. I smiled and removed the warming cover from the omelets in the center of the table.

I was glad Gordy was with Katie. He was so happy, he practically glowed. The emo kid from senior year was now replaced with a tanned, confident guy who never stopped smiling. It was a good look for him.

"Hey guys," I said. "You don't need the ninja stealth. I'm awake."

"And you cooked breakfast!" Katie said. "Something smells amazing."

"Omelets for us and a tofu and veggie scramble for Emma if she shows up hungry," I said, waving at the table. "Bon appetite."

Gordy grinned from ear to ear and I heard his stomach rumble from across the room. He never ate before surfing, so I knew he'd be starving. After smelling this stuff cook all morning, I was pretty hungry myself.

"Let me just change out of my wetsuit," he said. "I'll be right back."

Katie looked at Gordy and blushed. He was standing by the kitchen door in his wetsuit which was zipped open down to his hips, exposing a lot of tanned skin. He'd already removed his rash guard and had it tossed over one shoulder. I followed the swish swish sound of sandy feet and when he'd reached the master bathroom, I turned to Katie and winked.

"So things are good with you and the Gordster?" I asked.

I hadn't spent much time alone with Katie lately, and judging by the blushing that now made her freckles stand out, things were going very well indeed. Either that or she was embarrassed that I'd caught her ogling my friend's butt.

"Um, yes, Gordy's awesome," she said.

She twirled one of her auburn curls around one finger with a dreamy look on her face. The girl had it bad. Did I look that goofy when I talked about Cal? Yeah, I probably did.

"Good," I said. "He looks really happy."

"Who looks happy?" Gordy asked.

He walked into the kitchen in a pair of knee length board-shorts, graphic tee, and flip-flops. Gordy still wore his dark hair in an asymmetrical cut, but it had been tousled with a towel, giving him a devil-may-care look. He gave Katie a kiss on the cheek and smiled at the table full of food.

"Me," Katie squeaked. "I'm starving."

"Food makes us happy," I said. "Dig in."

I didn't have to tell him twice. We all piled our plates high with omelets, fried tomatoes, and toast. While we ate, Gordy and Katie filled me in on local gossip and I shared the latest progress on my art opening.

"So, are you working on more sketches today?" Gordy asked.

"Yeah," I said. "I need more small pieces. The market stall isn't huge, but it's taking me forever to fill it. I don't want it to look empty opening day."

"Anything we can do to help?" he asked.

"Nope," I said. "I even remembered to check the tide chart."

I held up my hand where I'd penned today's high and low tides. The local tide chart was one of the first things I checked online this morning, right after seeing if I had any messages from Cal. There were no new messages, but I wasn't worried. He was probably just busy with the wolf pack.

"Well, I know one thing we can do to help," Katie said. "Go ahead and get sketching, Gordy and I will take care of the dishes."

Gordy mock groaned, but he started stacking our dirty plates while Katie reached for the empty coffee mugs.

"You sure?" I asked.

I winced as my gaze fell on greasy pans and empty egg cartons. I'd made a huge mess of the kitchen while cooking, but if Katie wanted to clean up, I wasn't going to argue.

"Absolutely!" Katie said.

I smiled and grabbed my messenger bag, double checking that I had my cell phone and that it was fully charged. I wouldn't make the mistake of leaving it behind again. I also had my sketchbook and charcoals, but I wasn't really planning on creating any new art today.

"See you guys later," I said. "Give me a call if Emma or Cal show up."

"Sure thing," Gordy said.

I opened the creaky screen door and stepped down onto white sand. I headed back toward the rocky cove, but I wasn't going there to sketch the sea cliffs. I was on a hunt for ghosts.

Chapter 12

I figured that the ghosts of Sam and his band of not-so-merry-men would be strongest back at the cove where I'd first seen them manifest. My hunch was right. Sam sat on a rock, gazing out to sea. The motley group of Grays stood guard at his back.

The cove was empty except for me and my new, stinky friends. Sam didn't smell too bad, but the gunpowder smell of one the Grays made my nose itch. A familiar ache behind my eyes joined my itching nose, but I strode forward.

"Hey," I said, stopping in front of Sam. He'd risen from the rock and removed his hat. Standing face to face, I realized he wasn't much taller than me, and I was freaky short. I guess guys just weren't that tall back in the day.

Sam may not have towered over me, but the guy had presence. If I wasn't standing next to him, I'd have guessed the pirate was, like, seven feet tall. I wondered again why I could see him at all. How was he powerful enough to make himself, and his companions, visible? Was it because he had a particularly vital bit of unfinished business? But he'd mentioned treasure. How could finding pirate treasure be all that important?

I just shook my head. It's not like there's a guidebook for sensing the dead. Maybe seeing came naturally after smelling and I'd be seeing all ghosts this clearly from now on. I wasn't sure how I felt about that. Seeing floaty, glowy things was weird enough.

"Um, so how do we find this treasure?" I asked.

Sam started down the beach toward the jetty where I'd spent the previous evening. When he reached the rocks, he beckoned for me to join him. I shrugged and followed, keeping to the dry sand, the Grays at my back.

Goosebumps pricked the skin along my neck and scalp, but I focused on following Sam over algae slick rocks. If I dwelled on the creepy Grays lurking behind me, I'd chicken out. Thankfully, the climb up and over the jetty required all of my attention.

When I reached the top, I noticed another small pile of rocks on the side of the jetty opposite the cove. There was something white as clam shells at the highest point of the miniature island, but the shape was all wrong. It looked like a rock sitting atop a bundle of pale, white sticks. I swallowed hard and turned to Sam's ghost.

Sam continued down toward the rocks and turned to wave me on. Great. Ghosts may not get wet, but I'd have to wade through about two feet of water to get over to those rocks and their macabre booty. I sat and removed my boots before climbing down.

I fumbled with the laces and tried to keep my eyes averted from the rocks below. I was pretty sure I knew what Sam wanted to show me—and it wasn't treasure. I'd seen human bones once before and I wasn't keen to repeat the experience. But if I wanted to help Sam, and rid myself of smelly ghost pirates, I'd have to go examine those bones and whatever else waited down there.

I pulled off my striped stockings, stuffing them into the toes of my boots. A breeze blew off the water to tickle my toes and brushed along my tattooed ankle. Seeing the spirit tattoo made me think of Cal. I hoped he'd be able to make it to the beach house today. I couldn't talk to Gordy or Katie about ghosts—they had no idea that any of this paranormal stuff existed—and I was starting to feel like I was in way over my head. It would be nice to be able to run all of this by Cal. I could sure use his calm, level-headed perspective on Sam and his not-so-merry men.

I flicked my eyes to a scowling, toothless Gray and shivered. I considered calling Cal, but shook my head. He was busy with pack business. I could handle this, for now. I'd just take a look at what Sam wanted to show me and leave the rest until Cal or Emma returned. I sighed and started climbing down the rocks, trying not to think about what creepy things I might step on with bare feet.

At the bottom, I faced about three yards of ocean between me and the rocks where Sam stood, floated, whatever. Unlike the ghost I was following, I couldn't walk on water and it was way too far to jump across. I was going to have to get wet. I dipped a toe in the ocean and grimaced. The water was cold as the grave and just as inviting.

I took an involuntary step back and the rock where I stood wobbled. I reached out and caught myself from falling, but not before slicing my finger open on a cluster of barnacles. *Son of a dung beetle.* I hissed at the pain and stuck the finger in my mouth, sucking off the blood. When I pulled my finger away to look at it, the bleeding had stopped, but it throbbed with pain, matching my heartbeat. *Gross.*

I put a hand to my stomach and regretted the huge veggie omelet I'd wolfed down for breakfast. If I kept thinking about my pulsing finger, I'd probably end up puking, so I focused on the waves lapping at the rocks.

The water looked deeper from down here and I considered turning back and waiting for Cal after all. What the heck was I doing climbing over rocks and considering a swim to Bone Island? It's not like I was Laura Croft, though I could totally use her bull whip right now.

A large wave crashed on the rocks at my feet and sprayed me from head to toe. Heck, if I was already wet, I might as well get on with it. Plus, I was not going to let this beach win again. It had stranded me here for hours and had already drawn first blood. I narrowed my eyes at the ocean and waded in.

I'd made it over to the rocks when I saw something out of the corner of my eye. I flinched as a shadow danced across the rocks. A seagull swooped down low, taunting me with its cries, and I froze. What would the creature do to protect its nest? I'd seen what Hitchcock thought birds were capable of and I wasn't eager to find out if real life was as terrifying as fiction. In my life, reality was usually way scarier.

"Don't worry bird," I muttered. "I'm not here to steal eggs from your nest."

No, I had other treasure in mind. I was searching for the bones of Black Sam Bellamy, Prince of Pirates. Too bad the bird wasn't convinced.

I ducked my head against the bird's aggressive flight maneuvers and pushed myself into action, resuming my struggle to scale the mass of green and gray stone that loomed before me. Cold saltwater tugged at my skirt, threatening with the crash of every wave to tear my grasp from the seaweed-slick rocks and pull me down into the churning depths.

I dug fingernails painted with chipped, black polish into a narrow crevice and tried not to think about what might be lurking there. The razor-sharp barnacles were bad enough. I was already bleeding from my first encounter with the evil crustaceans. If I started worrying about what else lurked in the tide pools and rock crevices, it wouldn't be long before my imagination took over and I'd likely see dorsal fins cut through the surface of nearby waves.

I shook my head, wet hair slapping against my face. No, I wouldn't succumb to panic. There'd be plenty of time later to worry about sharks, jellyfish, and flying monkeys. For now, I had to focus on getting out of this water before the ocean swallowed me whole.

I wedged a bare foot into the space between two stones and, with a grunt, pulled myself up onto a pile of rocks. I sat dripping water and gasping for air like a fish flung onto shore. I grabbed and twisted my skirt with both hands, wringing water onto the rocks, and surveyed the area where I sat.

I was surrounded by tide pools that hovered just above the waves, at the base of a tall cliff. Of course, that would change soon enough. These rocks would be well beneath the ocean waters once the tide came in. It was no wonder that no one had discovered the pirate's remains before now. Only a madman or a fool would come out here in search of treasure.

So what did that make me?

I stood on wobbly legs and tried to clench my teeth against their chattering. The rocks looked different than they had from above and it took me a few minutes to get my bearings. I needn't have worried; the bones were easy to find. All I had to do was turn in a circle and look for Sam's ghost.

Sam stood over the skeletal remains, his sad eyes beckoning me forward. The Grays stood to either side, each wearing an identical grimace. I tried to keep the surprise off my face, but I felt my eyes widen. I'd been so focused on the squawking bird overhead and following Sam's ghost that I hadn't seen the surly, gray ghosts circle around me.

More than one of the Grays rested a hand on a pistol or blade and I shivered at their menacing presence. Sam may have been an okay guy, for a pirate, but these ghosts were another story. How many innocent people had they killed with those weapons? Judging from the color of their auras, I'm guessing they took a lot of lives. My mouth went dry and I cleared my throat as I approached Sam.

"So, um, this must be weird for you," I said, gesturing toward the skeleton. "That is you, right?"

The ghost nodded and my head filled with his scent.

"How did you end up here?" I asked. "We're a long way from where your ship went down."

Sam raised an eyebrow and pointed at the waves crashing around us. Oh, right. I guess his body must have been swept up with the same storm that wrecked the *Whydah*, carrying it far from Mary Hallett and eventually depositing the remains here.

Sam knelt down on one knee and gestured toward the skeleton, his hand movements jerky and posture stiff. Apparently, the ghost was anxious for me to take a closer look. What could a pile of bones have to do with treasure? I wasn't sure what I'd find there, but I leaned forward searching the skeleton for clues.

The morning had been cloudy, but the sun broke through at that moment to shine on the small bones of the dead pirate's hand. The skeleton wore a ring that caught the light and seemed to blaze with fire. Was that the treasure?

A large ruby was in an elaborate, jeweled setting that looked more suited to a woman's hand. It seemed like an odd thing for a manly pirate captain to be wearing, but what did I know about pirate bling? Maybe this kind of thing was cool back in the day, a way of showing status and wealth like the golf ball sized diamonds that modern rappers wear.

"Am I supposed to take the ring?" I asked.

Sam nodded like a kid on a sugar high. I wiped my hands on my skirt and took a deep breath. I wasn't normally this squeamish. I enjoyed slasher flicks and low budget monster movies, but deep down I knew the blood in those films was just Kool-Aid and corn starch. It wasn't real. But the pale, yellowed bones in front of me were no cheap movie prop.

I swallowed hard and lifted the ringed finger with shaking hands. I bit my lip to hold in a squeak as my skin met cold bone. They seemed to carry the chill of death and the threat of the ocean's deep, icy waters. I shivered and hastily removed the ring, dropping the bone to the rocks with a clatter.

Thankfully, Sam didn't seem to mind the clumsy handling of his remains. The ghost nodded and started walking back across the water and up onto the jetty. He hadn't disappeared, so there must be more to his unfinished business than just finding the ring. Of course there was; ghosts were never that easy.

I sighed and turned to wade across the stretch of water, the ring clutched in my fist. The water had risen and I could see that I'd need both hands to keep my balance. My eyes flicked up to where I'd left my boots and bag on top of the jetty. Without my bag, I'd either have to place the ring in my skirt pocket or on my finger. Bile rose in my throat as I slid the cold ring onto my left hand. I didn't dare risk carrying it in my pocket, not with those rising waves. If I lost the ring in that water, I'd never find it again. I'd be plagued with smelly ghost pirates forever.

Thankfully, dudes from Sam's time must have had small hands. The ring fit me perfectly. I made my way through the water and up the face of the jetty without incident. When I reached the top, I dropped down onto the rocks and shoved wet feet into my boots. With a sigh, I pulled a long package from my messenger bag.

I slid the Ouija board out of the plastic grocery bag I'd wrapped it in and placed the open board on the rocks, setting the pointer in the middle. I suspected that Sam would have more spirit energy here where he'd first manifested. I was hopeful that he could sustain his side of the conversation longer than he had last night at the beach house.

"So, um, was this what you wanted me to find?" I asked, holding up the ring.

The pointer slid to YES and the air filled with the scent of excited ghost pirates. My eye twitched and I grit my teeth. I sure hoped we were nearly done with their ghostly unfinished business. It was time for some spirits to find their way into the light before my brain exploded.

"Cool, then we're done?" I asked.

I held my breath and waited for the ghost's response. The plastic pointer whooshed across the board to NO and I sighed. A headache pounded behind my right eye and I fought a wave of dizziness as Sam's ghost concentrated on telling me what he wanted. I leaned in, trying to follow the rapidly moving pointer without passing out.

Take the fawney to Eastham, Massachusetts.

"Fawney?" I asked.

The pirate's chest and shoulders rose and fell with a sigh I'd never hear. He pointed at my finger and began to spell it out for me. *Ring.* He wanted me to take the ring to Eastham?

"What's in Eastham?" I asked.

My dearest treasure.

Okay, so we were back to treasure. Good to know. I rocked back on my heels and sighed. Looks like I had a road trip in my near future.

"Anywhere specific I should start my search when I reach Eastham?" I asked.

The Devil's Cliff, Lucifer Land.

"Yeah, that sounds like a fun place," I muttered.

My phone chirped and I jumped. I dug through my bag to check the text message. There was a message from Simon saying that he and Cal were on their way to the beach house and they were bringing pizza. I smiled and pocketed the phone.

"So, anything else you can tell me about this treasure?" I asked.

But when I turned to where the pirates had floated just moments before, they weren't there.

"Oka-a-a-y, that's not creepy or anything," I said, turning in a slow circle.

My eyes searched the rocks and approaching waves, but the pirates were gone. I shrugged and starting packing up the Ouija board. The ring on my finger caught the light and I paused to admire the blood red gemstones.

With a sigh—it really was pretty—I removed the ring, wrapped it in a napkin, and secured it within the inside zipper pocket of my messenger bag. With a bounce in my step, despite the nightmares of the previous night, I headed back to the beach house. I couldn't wait to see Cal. If I closed my eyes, I could still feel the warm, urgent pressure of his kisses on my lips. My skin tingled and a flutter rose in my chest at the memory.

My eyes flicked to where a ghost of the moon hovered on the horizon. It was three days past the full moon, time enough for Cal to have gained control over his wolf. I licked my lips and shivered in anticipation. *We have unfinished business Calvin Miller.*

I raised a hand to my lips as they lifted into a slow smile. I was hungry for something all right, but it wasn't the promise of food that had my boots running down the beach. I ran past startled tourists, grinning from ear to ear. I'd missed Cal and his swoon-worthy kisses. Pizza would have to wait.

Chapter 13

I raced up the back steps of the beach house, taking them two at a time. I made a beeline through the house to the front porch, the screen door I'd flung open in haste slamming shut behind me. I'd passed Gordy and Katie on the beach, pausing only to wave as I made my way up to the house. That meant I had at least a few precious minutes of alone time with Cal.

Too bad I'd forgotten about Simon. I grinned like a dork and ran out onto the porch, expecting to find Cal coming up the drive. Instead, I rushed headlong into a tall werewolf wearing a leather jacket and an annoying smirk that tugged at the edges of the scar that crossed his handsome face. *Oof.* Running into Simon was like smashing into a brick wall—a very, very annoying brick wall. I stepped back, rubbed my forehead, and sighed.

"Where's Cal?" I asked.

"Nice to see you too, Love," Simon said.

"Hello, Simon," I said, teeth clenched. "Wow, it is so awesome to be in your amazing presence." Now that the social niceties were out of the way, I rolled my eyes at Simon and crossed my arms. "So where's Cal?"

"Just grabbing a few essentials from the truck," he said, waving a hand back toward the road.

Right. Simon's motorcycle was leaning on its kickstand in the shade of the porch, but Cal would have brought his truck which would have to be parked out by the main road. The driveway to the beach house wasn't much more than a footpath. Emma's compact car had been a tight squeeze, which meant Cal's truck would never fit.

I stepped forward, ready to push past Simon and go help Cal with whatever he was carrying from the truck. But at that moment Cal stepped into sight and his arms were laden with something other than pizza boxes.

Cal's arms were wrapped around a pretty girl in a tight fitting cami and cut off shorts. She had an athletic build and was tall, with long arms and legs tanned bronze from the sun. Her chin length, light brown hair covered her eyes, and she had a cute round face and button nose. I disliked her immediately.

"You should wipe that jealous expression off your face, love," Simon said. "It doesn't suit you."

I glared at Simon, but our stare down was short-lived. My head swung back to face the spectacle of Cal with his arms around another woman. I wanted to tear my eyes away, but couldn't resist the gravitational pull. It was like this moment defined my future and I was a piece of space debris, swept along wherever Planet Cal chose to take me. I didn't like the feeling, not one bit.

Simon, who was still standing just off my right shoulder, popped the top of a soda can and I flinched. I was so tightly wound that it was amazing the sudden movement didn't break something. I needed to chill out.

I took a deep breath and tried to be rational. There was no reason to jump to crazy conclusions. Cal was a nice guy. He was probably just comforting that totally cute girl with the perfect hair and athletic body.

The sound of my teeth grinding could be heard over Simon who was noisily slurping soda. The accompanying pain in my jaw jolted me from my torturous thoughts. *Oh em gees*, Simon was right. I was jealous.

Simon cleared his throat as Cal and the girl, still arm in arm, walked closer. I pasted a smile on my face and stepped down to meet them in the gravel strewn driveway.

"Hi!" I said, waving to the new girl.

Okay, maybe that was just a bit too perky. If I kept this up, people would think I was impersonating Katie.

"Hey," she said. The girl lifted her head and pretty, green eyes surveyed the house. Yep, even her eyes were gorgeous. "You were right, Cal. This place is agreeable."

My smile faltered as her low, sultry voice said Cal's name like they were long lost besties or…or lovers.

"This is London," Cal said. "She's the new werewolf I was telling you about."

Right, this was the kid who was going through her first change. For some reason, I hadn't imagined the werewolf to look like this London girl.

"You don't sound British," I said. I bit my lip and looked away. *Open mouth, insert foot much, Yuki?*

"I'm not," she said. "I'm from Wolfborough."

"A werewolf from Wolfborough, Maine?" I asked.

"Yeah, my parents are big into the irony," she said. "Just like my name. London means fortress of the moon."

London rolled her eyes and blushed, which just made her look cuter. Part of me wanted to hate her for that, but I could relate to not liking my name. Plus, there was something fragile lingering just below her perfect exterior.

"Right, 'cause living in Wolfborough wasn't a big enough tip off," I said.

"It could be worse," she said with a shrug. "My sister's name is Luna."

"That's not so bad," I said. "It's kind of pretty."

"Tell that to my kid sister," she said. "Her classmates call her Luna the lunatic."

"That sucks," I said. "Kids are cruel."

That was an understatement.

"London's staying with us until her parents get back from New York City," Cal said.

"Oh, are they there on vacation or something?" I asked.

I almost felt bad for London at that moment. If I were a werewolf with a werekid going through her first change, I'd want to be there to help her through it all. I certainly wouldn't be chillaxing in the Big Apple.

"No, they're working," she said with a shrug. "My mom and dad will be at the loft until next week. That's the apartment they share with their fellow thespians."

"Your parents are lesbians?" I asked.

I knew I was missing something, but my brain was still muddled from Cal's continued proximity to London's svelte body and tanned arms and legs. My frustration grew as they shared a look and giggled.

"*Thespians*, not lesbians," London said.

"London's parents are actors," Cal said. "They had to return to work after the full moon."

"Our considerate alpha volunteered to take London under his wing," Simon said, grinning at my discomfort. *Jerk.*

"So what do you do around here for fun?" London asked.

She stepped forward, moving with the poise of a dancer and the predatory grace of a wolf—until she placed weight on her left ankle and winced. Cal caught her up in his arms again and I fought down the urge to rip her from his grasp. Couldn't Simon step in and be the knight in shining armor?

"Long walks on the beach," Simon said with a wink. "But you won't be doing any of that until that ankle fully heals."

I looked down to see London's ankle wrapped in an ace bandage that I hadn't noticed until now. A mottling of blue and purple spread out from her ankle and down to the top of her foot. Since werewolves are gifted with rapid healing, she'd either hurt herself pretty bad, or this injury was recent.

"What happened?" I asked.

"My foot got caught in my clothes during an involuntary shift," she said. "Cal didn't get my clothes off fast enough that time."

That time? So Cal's been taking this girl's clothes off, more than once? My eyes widened until I thought they might pop out of my head.

London shrugged and Cal's hand slid from her shoulder to her bare arm. I bit the inside of my cheek. *I will not be jealous. I will not be jealous. I will not be jealous.*

At least Cal had the good sense to look embarrassed.

"I-I-I didn't look or anything," he said, holding a hand up. "London's just having some trouble controlling her wolf."

"And you decided to bring her *here*?" I asked. "Why on earth would you do that? In case you've forgotten, Gordy and Katie don't know anything about werewolves."

They didn't know about ghosts either and I'd brought a pack of ghost pirates into the house last night. Did that make me a hypocrite? No. Ghosts can't hurt our innocent friends, but a wild, out of control werewolf could.

"Don't worry, Love," Simon said. "Cal and I will stay close to London. Your friends will remain safe."

That was what I was afraid of. Maybe I didn't want Cal sticking close to London. I sighed and turned to go inside.

"I thought you'd be happy to see me," Cal said. "Simon and I were missing you and Emma. That's why we came to the beach house. But if you want us to leave, we will."

As much as I wanted London gone, I liked the idea of Cal spending another day with her at wolf camp even less. I turned back to give Cal a rueful smile and put my hands on my hips.

"I didn't say you had to leave," I said. "I just think we need to be careful. I don't want anyone getting hurt." Oh, I meant that in so many different ways.

"Thanks," Cal said.

"So where's the pizza you guys promised?" I asked.

Pizza usually made everything better, but I wasn't so sure that yummy cheese and tomato sauce could slay the green-eyed monster that gripped my heart in its pointy claws. But I was willing to give pizza a chance. I'd never felt jealousy over Cal before and I wasn't enjoying the experience. It was becoming hard to breath with anger, guilt, and embarrassment waging war inside my chest.

"Here, I'll show you," Cal said. "The pizza's out in my truck. Simon, can you help London inside?"

"Right, I always do love a beautiful woman on my arm," Simon said, sauntering down the steps toward London. He bowed theatrically, a grin touching his lips. "Welcome to the beach house."

Simon held out his hand and helped London up the porch steps. I walked over to where Cal stood waiting for me. One hand was shoved into the front pocket of his low-slung jeans, tugging the faded denim even lower on his hips. He ran the fingers of his other hand through his hair and his shirt lifted, revealing an inch of bare skin. Warmth filled my chest and it had nothing to do with anger or jealousy.

Cal cleared his throat, his posture rigid. With an effort, I stopped ogling the hard muscles of Cal's stomach and looked up into his cerulean blue eyes. His handsome face was marred by the hint of a frown, but when I stepped forward to take his hand, he pulled me close.

"I'm sorry about bringing London here," he said.

I sighed into his chest, wishing we could stay like this. Why did there have to be pretty weregirls, annoying pack lieutenants, and smelly ghosts?

"I'm sorry too," I said. "Holy jealousy, Batman. That was big time awkward."

"You were jealous?" Cal asked.

I looked up to see his eyebrows reach beneath his hair. I thought my raging jealousy had been obvious—it had been to Simon—but maybe Cal was just worried about my reaction to bringing an unstable werewolf into our home away from home. London's lack of control was something I was worried about too, but mostly I was irritated that my boyfriend had shown up with his arm around another girl.

"Hugely, massively, über jealous," I said.

Cal leaned down, his lips brushing mine before he pulled away to look into my eyes. His thumb traced the sensitive skin along my jaw, sending shivers down my spine.

"You have nothing to be jealous about," he said. "I am all yours, forever."

I liked the sound of that.

"Promise?" I asked.

"I promise," he said.

Tangling my fingers in Cal's hair, I pulled him closer. The cool brush of Cal's lips was replaced by a solar flare of heat as I kissed him, letting him feel the storm of emotions swirling around inside of me. Eventually, our kisses became less urgent and we parted with matching grins.

"We should argue more often," I said.

"Were we arguing?" he asked.

"Not really, but maybe we should," I said, tilting my head to the side. "Just imagine the make-up kissing if we had a real fight."

"You should definitely give it a try," Emma said.

I turned to see my best friend walking down the path toward us. We hadn't made it out to Cal's truck yet, otherwise I might have noticed Emma drive up. *Maybe.* I was a bit distracted.

Emma would know all about the thrill of make-up kissing. She and Simon argued all the time. I shook my head, trying to dispel the image of those two making out. I'd see enough of the real thing soon enough.

I broke away from Cal's embrace, but continued to hold his hand. I'd missed him way too much the past few days to let go.

"If you want to fight and make up with Simon, he's inside," Cal said.

Emma smiled and hurried down the path. We followed a few minutes later, stacks of cooling pizza in our arms. As Cal and I made our way up the porch steps, Emma's voice bellowed out the front door that still hung open.

"Who the hell is SHE?" Emma snapped.

Son of a dung beetle. Emma had met London and was having a similar, if more vocal, reaction to my own.

We walked in to see Emma pointing at London and staring daggers at Simon who still had his arm around the weregirl's waist. I chuckled and walked toward the kitchen. We all needed some pizza therapy.

"I see you've met London," I said over my shoulder. "Come on, let's eat."

Emma raised an eyebrow and looked from Simon to me. Simon, a former playboy with a bad reputation, looked more startled than guilty. Too bad, for the first time ever, he was also at a loss for words. I shook my head and continued on into the kitchen.

With a shrug and a sigh, Emma followed. We'd been friends forever and she knew I'd never take Simon's side over her own. If I was suggesting food, then everything was normal. Well, as normal as things got around here.

I grabbed a slice of veggie pizza and ate while Cal made the introductions and explained about his decision to bring London here from Wolf Camp. Emma nodded, but I could tell from the gleam in her eye that she and Simon were having some of that hot, make-up kissing later. *Gag.*

I set down my pizza and pushed the plate away. I was already having a hard time trying to eat with a room full of smelly ghosts. It was bad enough that The Grays were ogling Emma and London, but Sam's haunting presence made my stomach twist in knots. The ghost stared at me with sad eyes, trapped here on this plane until I helped him with his unfinished business.

I turned and looked out the window to see Gordy still riding waves, Katie cheering him on. We needed to go let our friends know we were all here, but first, I had to bring everyone up to speed on our other house guests.

Cal wasn't the only one to have brought home strays. Mine may not be ridiculously cute and hog all the sausage pizza, but I had a feeling my friends wouldn't be too happy about sharing the beach house with the ghosts of murderous pirates.

I wasn't wrong.

Chapter 14

"They're here?" London asked. "Like right now?"

Her eyes flicked around the room, looking for signs of ghost pirates. But since she was just a werewolf, she couldn't sense spirits of the dead. *Geesh*, you know your life is far from normal when you think things like, "just a werewolf."

"Yeah, the guy with no teeth likes you," I said. "He keeps trying to sniff your hair."

London squeaked and moved away from the kitchen counter—and closer to Cal. Gumby smiled, the ghost showing off his lack of teeth in all his gingivitis glory, and I stifled a shudder. Maybe I shouldn't have shared what the Grays were doing, even to our annoying house guest. But she did ask.

"Banish them or whatever it is you do," she said.

London put her hands on her hips and glared at me. What? It's not like I set the ghost on her tail.

"I can't," I said.

"Why not?" she asked, rolling her eyes.

"Because I don't control them," I said.

"Then what good are you?" she asked.

I bit the inside of my cheek and tamped down a scream. I so did not want to get into a cat fight, especially with an unstable werewolf, but London was getting on my last nerve.

"Yuki's not some dead people puppet master," Emma said. "She's much more important than that. She has the power to lead lost spirits into the light."

"Well, then do your creepy, Pied Piper thing and lead these ghosts into the light already," London said, turning to stare down her nose at me.

I sighed and shook my head.

"It's not that simple," I said. "I have to help Sam with some unfinished business."

"Sam?" she asked.

London looked at me like I'd grown three heads. What was so weird about calling a ghost by his first name?

"Yes, Black Sam Bellamy," I said. "You know, the pirate captain? He wants me to bring his ring to a place called the Devil's Cliff in Eastham, Massachusetts. It's down around Cape Cod."

I knew that much from my previous search on the pirate. Now I just had to convince my friends to take me and car full of ghost pirates to Cape Cod.

"Are we really going in search of pirate treasure?" Cal asked with a toothy grin on his face.

"I've seen this movie," Emma said, shaking her head. "It doesn't end well."

"No, Love," Simon said. "But it's bound to be interesting."

"So, road trip?" I asked.

Since I don't have a car—driving really isn't safe when ghosts pop in whenever they feel like it—I was relying on my friends to help me finish this job leading the ghosts into the light. I couldn't do this on my own.

"To hunt for pirate treasure with my beautiful girlfriend?" Cal asked. "Absolutely."

"I'm always in the mood to hunt for booty," Simon said with a wink.

Emma punched him on the arm and shook her head. I just rolled my eyes at Simon. I had no idea how Emma put up with the man.

"I'm in," she said. "Someone has to keep these knuckleheads in line."

I grinned and turned to London. I'd rather leave the girl behind, but if she was having trouble controlling her wolf, she was coming with. No way was she staying here with Gordy and Katie.

"Sure, fine, whatever," she said. "Maybe I can find a rabbit to eat or something. It's not like there's anything to do here at the beach. Seagulls are boring."

I grit my teeth, and Emma and I exchanged a look. No bunnies, or seagulls, would be harmed during this road trip. Not over our dead bodies.

"She's kidding," Cal said. "Right, London?"

Cal's wolf slipped behind his eyes and London tilted her head to the side, exposing her neck in what I'd come to learn was a submissive move. Cal was pack alpha, which meant his word was law. If he didn't want her going furry and eating bunnies, then London would have to obey. That was good, since Emma would seriously put the hurt on if someone tried to harm an innocent bunny rabbit.

I interrupted, hastily changing the subject.

"We just need to make one pit stop so I can run a quick errand along the way," I said.

I tried to use my best no-big-deal look, but nobody was buying it. Maybe I needed more practice.

"This errand wouldn't involve a detour through Salem, would it?" Emma asked.

"Um, yeah," I said. "How'd you guess?"

Cal sighed and ran fingers through his hair.

"Are you sure?" he asked. "About the amulet?"

Huh, I guess everyone had figured out the reason for my little pit stop in Salem.

"Yes," I said. "Dead sure."

"It won't be easy, love," Simon said. "Those witches won't suffer a second break-in easily. They'll have beefed up security since our last trip inside their shop."

"Witches?" London asked. "What shop are we talking about? What's going on?"

"The Cauldron and Noose," I said. "We're going to Salem to return an amulet to its rightful owners."

"And these rightful owners are witches?" she asked.

"Well, yeah," I said. I picked at the edges of my nail polish, wishing London wasn't here for this.

"You stole from witches," she said. "Are you crazy?"

"Crazy like a fox," I said.

Simon snorted and Cal grinned and shook his head. Emma forced a smile and reached over to bump knuckles.

"Don't worry," Emma said. "We totally have your back."

I nodded, but I couldn't help but notice London's glare. I was pretty sure I didn't want to show that girl my back, not unless I wanted to give her a place to sink her claws.

Chapter 15

We joined Gordy and Katie down on the beach an hour later. The boys and London went for a swim, but Emma hung back with me and Katie.

"I don't like her," Katie said, watching London dive gracefully through the waves.

I tried not to gasp in surprise. Katie liked everyone. She was one of the happiest, nicest girls I'd ever met.

"She has that effect on people," I said.

"Females," Emma said. "She has that effect on females. Clueless males on the other hand..."

She gestured to the ocean where Gordy, Cal, and Simon followed London through the waves. They were like bewitched puppy dogs. Since two of them were werewolves, that actually wasn't a bad analogy. I snorted and Emma turned a questioning eyebrow my way.

"It's just...maybe she has some animal magnetism thing going on," I said.

Katie didn't know that paranormal stuff was real, so I couldn't say, "maybe it's because London's a werewolf." Emma's eyes narrowed as she turned her gaze back out to sea.

She wasn't the only one watching the water. Sam stood beside me, sad eyes roving the horizon. His stance reminded me of the stories I'd read about Mary Hallett keeping her vigil on the sea cliffs, waiting for Sam's return. When he someday made his way into the light, would Sam be reunited with his true love? For his sake, and the sake of Mary, I sure did hope so.

The raw pain on Sam's face was hard to bear, but it was preferable to watching the Grays leer at every woman in a bathing suit. You'd think they'd never seen a bikini before.

"I think it's because she's two-faced," Katie said.

"What do you mean?" I asked.

I leaned toward Katie and she blushed.

"It's just...one minute she acts all vulnerable and the next she's showing off how strong and athletic she is," Katie said.

Emma nodded.

"She's like sweet and sour tofu," Emma said.

"The guys don't like tofu," I said.

"You know what I mean," Emma said.

"Yeah, I do," I said with a sigh.

"I'm sick of watching The London Show," Emma said. "Think I'll catch up on some online petitions. That puppy mill in New Hampshire wasn't the first and, unfortunately, isn't the last."

"I'll come with," I said.

Maybe Emma could help me do some online reconnaissance of the Cauldron and Noose. My plan for returning Nera's amulet to the Salem witches was still pretty sketchy. So far it consisted of breaking in, swapping the fake amulet for the real amulet, and praying we don't get caught. As far as plans went, it was like facing the zombie apocalypse with a nail file and a bag of Skittles. It might work, but chances were good that I'd die a horrible, painful death.

At least the end would be filled with fruity, candy goodness. And for my dramatic death scene I could whisper, in a creepy, quivery death rattle, *taste the rainbow*. Boy would those zombies be confused.

"Katie?" Emma asked, pulling me out of my zombie fantasy. Katie shrugged.

"No, you guys go on back," she said. "I think I'll go for a swim after all."

Katie pulled off her shorts and ran into the ocean. I wish I was that brave, but a childhood viewing of Jaws had cured me of ever swimming for fun. Plus, there wasn't enough sunscreen in the world for me to run around in a bikini. I'd be burned to a crisp.

"You go girl," Emma said.

Katie was already at Gordy's side, wrapping her arms around his waist. London was showing off some water acrobatics, but when she surfaced Gordy and Katie were making out. London scowled and I turned toward the beach house with a smile. The weregirl had met her match.

Chapter 16

I fumbled with my phone, groaning as the chirping tones of the programmed alarm dug spikes into my skull. We'd stayed up late telling ghost stories around the fire pit. Gordy had wanted to have a beach bonfire party now that we were all here and Katie came up with the idea of telling ghost stories. That girl was brilliant. She spent the entire night clinging to her boyfriend. Katie was my new hero.

Of course, London didn't miss a chance to seek comfort from Cal and Simon. As the moon rose in the sky, the guys became more and more protective. If London had her way, she'd have spent the night in their laps. Emma and I took turns gritting our teeth in between snuggles with our boyfriends.

I ran my tongue along my teeth, surprised they weren't worn down to little nubs. At least I hadn't been haunted by my usual recurring nightmare involving the Salem witches killing everyone I loved. I took that as a good sign. Maybe I could get in and out of the Cauldron and Noose without a hitch. *Yeah, right.*

"Get up," Emma said, pulling the covers back. "We have a long day of treasure hunting and B and E."

"Oooh, I can't wait to use my ninja skills," I said, yawning.

"Wearing black doesn't make you a ninja," she said.

"Sure it does," I said. "I can slip into the shadows like, well, a shadow."

It was too early in the morning for witty banter.

"Good luck with that," Emma said. "There won't be many dark shadows at high noon, which is when we'll be driving through Salem."

Son of a dung beetle. I hadn't thought of that. Not that my not-so-foolproof plan was entirely my fault. I hadn't had a lot of time to figure out the specifics.

I tried to mentally adapt my plan to daylight hours. Huh, if we stopped at the Cauldron and Noose during the day, I wouldn't have to break in. I could just waltz through the doors and leave the amulet in the display case for the witches to find, easy peasy. Maybe this wouldn't be so bad after all.

"Hey, cross breaking and entering off our to-do list," I said.

"Really?" Emma asked.

She held her breath and leaned forward with a smile. Too bad I was about to turn that smile upside down.

"I'm still getting rid of the amulet," I said. "I just don't think I have to break in like a thief in the night, since, you know, it will be during the day."

"Oh," Emma said, gravity winning the struggle with her lips.

It was a weighty "oh." Good thing I was still flat on my back in bed. In fact, maybe I'd just pull up the covers and let myself recover from the onslaught. Too bad Emma disagreed with that plan. She tugged back the blankets and tossed them on the floor.

"Why are you harshing on my plan?" I groaned.

"Which plan are we talking about?" Emma asked. "The plan to sleep all day or the plan to give away your best shot at surviving Samhain."

I rolled myself onto the edge of the bed and rubbed my eyes. This wasn't the first time we'd had this conversation, but if I managed to stash Nera's amulet at the occult shop in Salem, it should be our last. Even so, if I couldn't sleep, I preferred to argue facing my opponent.

With a heavy sigh, I pulled myself onto my feet and stuffed them into Jack Skellington slippers. I looked down into Jack's glowering face. He looked like I felt, irritated and half dead.

"Fine, I'm out of bed," I said. "See, I'm not going to sleep all day."

"But you are planning on returning the amulet to the witches," she said.

I started pacing the length of the room, hands fisted at my sides.

"You know I don't have a choice," I said. "I told you about the dreams."

"There's always a choice, Yuki," Emma said. "And I don't think you're making the right one. What if the dreams don't mean anything? They could just be your subconscious mind working through the guilt of stealing something."

"No," I said, shaking my head. "I can't take that chance. I won't let my actions be the reason you all get hurt."

"But..." she said.

I held up my hand, cutting off her words.

"Even if it is just a silly dream," I said. "I don't think I need the amulet anymore. My ghost sensing powers are stronger now. I can see their auras without wearing the amulet. Heck, I can see Sam and his posse like they're flesh and blood."

Transparent flesh and blood, but it was still way more than I could see last week.

"But the legend said that the amulet helped to protect the wearer on Samhain, not just be able to see spirits of the dead," she said.

"I've got that covered too," I said. "I've helped lots of ghosts since last Samhain. I'll have my own army of spirits to help defend me."

"I don't think an old farmer, a minister, an accountant, and a teenage girl constitute an army," Emma said, flashing me a dubious grin.

"Hey!" I said. "If we help Sam and his Gray buddies into the light, I'll have swashbuckling pirates fighting for me next Samhain. I'm guessing that pirates can kick butt."

Emma rolled her eyes.

"You're not changing your mind, are you?" she asked.

"Nope," I said.

"Fine," she said. "It's your funeral. Let's go make our excuses to Gordy and Katie."

"We're about to make Katie's day," I said.

"How's that?" Emma asked, raising an eyebrow.

"She's about to learn that London's parents have called and asked us to take her to Cape Cod to check on storm damage to their summer house," I said. "While we're actually off solving my witch and ghost pirate problems, Katie will have Gordy all to herself for the entire day. This road trip is a win-win."

I tried to sound confident, but I wasn't so sure that returning the amulet was the smartest thing. I just knew it was the right thing. I chewed my lip and waited for the vampire bats to stop having an epic battle in my stomach.

Chapter 17

"Are we there yet?" London asked for the millionth time. She was worse than a toddler hyped up on pixie sticks.

"No," Emma said through clenched teeth.

Her white-knuckled fingers gripped the steering wheel tight and I sighed. Someone ought to diffuse the situation before we drove off a bridge. Speaking of...

"Son of a dung beetle," I squeaked. "Where'd that bridge come from?"

I climbed off Cal's lap to crouch down on the floorboards of Emma's car. I squeezed my eyes shut and tried practicing a mental exercise my therapist had taught me. I counted in my head as cute zombie squirrels leapt over a bright, blue river. The game was supposed to help calm my nerves when I got angry or anxious in response to threatening situations. After my abduction this spring, I'd had some trouble controlling my emotions. We'd started with penguins, but found that zombie squirrels held my attention longer.

But as the car rumbled over the bridge the squirrel lost his balance and fell into the river. My eyes flew open to see London sneering at me from where she sat beside Cal in the back seat. I tried to respond with a death glare of my own, but my position at London's feet made things awkward. Oh well, at least she was no longer annoying our driver. Emma could thank me later.

A warm hand rested on my back and Cal bent forward.

"You okay?" he asked. "We're past the bridge now."

Oh, that was fast.

"Really?" I asked. "That thing was huge."

"What is wrong with you?" London asked. "All we did was cross a tiny bridge. What kind of freak goes fetal about a bridge?"

"Are you calling me a freak?" I asked.

It was a sore spot. I'd been called a freak, and worse, all through school. Now that I'd finally graduated, I was sick of it. I'd hoped that no one would ever call me names again. Oh well. If wishes were flying monkeys, we'd all be wearing tiny hats. I pulled myself up onto my knees and glared at London, hands fisting at my sides.

"Everyone has something they're afraid of," Cal said.

He was staring at London and the growl of his wolf slipped into his voice. London turned to Cal, eyebrows raised.

"Even you?" she asked.

"Even me," he said his face grave.

"You're pack alpha," she said. "What can you possibly be afraid of?"

"Seeing the girl you just called a freak hurting," he said.

London gulped and pushed into her seat, edging away from Cal.

"Um, sorry Yuki," she said, eyes downcast.

"No problem," I said. "Just don't do it again. You don't know me and have no right to judge me."

I settled onto Cal's lap and watched fields of cows and hay bales fly by. It wasn't long before the fields were replaced by billboards and warehouses. Emma turned off the highway, taking one of the exits to Salem. My fingers gripped the amulet in my pocket and I took a deep breath. Bridges and flying monkeys weren't the only things I was afraid of.

But before we entered downtown Salem, where my adventure to return the amulet would begin, we hit road construction. Signs pointed us to a detour and my heart began to race.

"Are you alright?" Cal asked.

"It can't be," I said.

"Bloody hell," Simon said. "Turn around, love. We can't go this way."

"What?" Emma asked, squinting at the traffic inching its way past orange cones. "Why not?"

"That's why," I said, pointing a shaking finger at a sign that was half covered by an overgrown bush.

A mew of terror escaped my lips and Cal's arms tightened around me. The sign read Salem Cemetery. That place and I had an unpleasant history. I had to avoid it at all cost.

"What gives?" London asked. "You're, like, the Ghost Whisperer. So why are you so freaked out? It's just a cemetery. Aren't ghosts your thing?"

Damn, that girl just didn't learn. The car filled with the scent of wet dog as Cal tried to control his anger. London wasn't making herself any friends on this road trip.

A crow alighted on the rock wall to our right. A second and third crow swooped past Emma's windshield to join their pal. There was a break in the wall where the crows had gathered and I noticed a narrow, hidden lane.

"Turn right there," I said. "Follow those birds."

I'd learned to follow crows. It was a wolf thing, but since I was an honorary pack member the noisy, black birds tended to help me out too. It was like they'd taken me under their wing. *Har, har.* But seriously, wolves and crows have a special relationship. In the wild, wolves will often follow crows to a food source. Crows have even been known to warn wolves of danger.

So when I spotted the crows, I knew they were here to lead us out of danger and away from the cemetery. I try to avoid places where the dead gather—cemeteries, graveyards, hospitals—due to how overwhelming the presence of so many angry ghosts can be, and very old cemeteries like this one were worse than most. Salem has a long, dark history and the ghosts who haunt that cemetery are filled with rage.

I bit my lip and kept my eyes averted from the cemetery as Emma turned the car onto the narrow lane. I wished I could help all those ghosts find peace, but not today. Someday I may become strong enough to face down those spirits, but if I tried to step foot beyond those walls of stone and wrought iron, I'd face an onslaught of angry ghosts that may very well scramble my brain. I wasn't ready to take that risk.

I felt the car come to a stop and I opened my eyes. I hadn't realized I'd closed them. I hoped that London hadn't noticed or I'd never hear the end of it. We were on a small side street lined with old trees. In fact, plants seemed to be taking over the entire block. In every yard rhododendron bushes and creeping ivy seemed to be swallowing the buildings whole.

"What's up?" I asked. "Why are we stopping?"

I inched away from the window as the breeze blew the branch of a willow tree to brush along the glass. This place gave me the creeps. I kept a watchful eye on a nearby overgrown rose bush. I half expected it to pucker its rosebud lips and demand, "Feed me, Seymour, feed me!" I blame my overactive imagination on the fact we were still within spitting distance of Salem Cemetery.

"I need to check a map," Emma said. "My GPS doesn't know where we are. I'm guessing not many people come down this lane."

I had to agree, since there were no other cars in sight. There were, however hundreds of crows. The birds were perched along both sides of the road, farther down the lane.

"I think we're supposed to keep going straight ahead," I said, pointing a shaky finger at the legion of beady eyes staring my way.

"No offense to the birds, but I'd prefer to check the map," she said.

Emma scanned the map on her phone and raised an eyebrow.

"What?" I asked. "Where are we according to the map?"

"Huh," she said, turning her phone so we could see. "This is a shortcut. If we keep going straight, we'll come out in downtown Salem near the municipal parking. Then it's just a short walk to the Cauldron and Noose."

"So this little detour actually saved us time?" London asked.

"Yes," Emma said.

She started the car and pulled back onto the street. We followed the crows into the popular Salem historic district. As soon as Emma parked the car, I jumped out and slung my messenger bag over my shoulder.

"I'll be right back," I said. "Wish me luck."

"You don't want us to go with you?" Cal asked.

I shook my head.

"This is something I need to take care of by myself," I said. "Plus, we don't all need to get in trouble. If I get caught putting the amulet back, they'll know I'm guilty. We don't all have to take the fall."

"What if we just wait outside?" Emma asked.

I bit my lip and considered the offer. In the dreams I'd had, the witches sought their revenge by hurting my friends. I didn't want any of them in harm's way. I started to shake my head in the negative, but Simon held up a hand.

"How about I act as lookout," he said. "If something goes wrong, I can get word to the others without everyone gawking from the street. It will be like old times."

Simon had helped me the first time I broke into the occult shop. And as much as I didn't want anything linking me to my friends, I could tell by Cal's rigid body that he was about to protest me going alone. Simon's offer was the best compromise.

"Okay," I said. "Simon can watch from the street corner like before. But I want the rest of you to wait here at the car. We might need to make a quick getaway."

Everyone reluctantly agreed. I'd tossed in the idea of making a quick getaway, but the truth was, if I got caught, I doubted the witches would let me escape. Running was not an option.

I pasted a smile on my face and nodded to Simon.

"Come on, old man," I said. "It's time to go make things right."

Chapter 18

Simon and I walked up Essex Street until we came within sight of the Cauldron and Noose. A huge, black cauldron sat in the shop window framed by a garland of rope looped into a series of nooses. I swallowed hard and surveyed the street.

Everything appeared normal, for Salem. Shoppers in street clothes and performers in costumes were bustling up and down the street, and food smells came from a nearby restaurant. Even the smell of ghost pirates—salt brine, rum, gun powder, and roasting meat—fit in here. The only thing out of place was the crows.

Hundreds of crows had landed on the rooftops lining the street, looking down from their perches like beady-eyed gargoyles. It was surreal. I half expected my dung beetle spirit guide to tunnel up through the cobblestone street, waking me from a dream. But this was no nightmare; I was really here, in Salem, returning Nera's amulet.

Simon continued past the occult shop and proceeded to flirt with a girl who was wearing a tight fitting pirate wench costume. The irony of seeing someone dressed as a pirate was not lost on me, though the costume most definitely was not historically accurate. I flicked my eyes to Sam Bellamy and his crew as they lumbered up the street. No way would these guys be caught dead, *giggle*, in that girl's frilly pirate get up.

Sam and The Grays had appeared as soon as I exited the car, popping into existence and making me squeak like a mouse. Their presence shouldn't have surprised me. Once a ghost, or in this case ghosts, find me, they never give up. No, these pirates would tag along until I helped them find their way into the light, no matter how long it takes.

The continued presence of the ghostly miscreants gave me even more motivation to get this job over with and be on our way to Cape Cod. The dead men moved closer and I winced. A pounding grew at my temples as my headache worsened. The strong smells emanating from each man wasn't helping.

I checked on Simon where he now leaned against the brick building on the corner, and nodded. I approached the occult shop under the watchful eyes of the gathered crows, and with a deep breath, stepped inside.

There was no one behind the counter and no shoppers in sight; the place was empty. I released the breath I was holding and tiptoed to the wood and glass case where I'd originally found the amulet.

There it was. The copy Simon's black market contact had made for me. The amulet that rested on plush velvet looked identical to the one in my pocket, but that's where the similarities ended. The original amulet could protect the wearer from the spirits who pierce the veil on Samhain, but the imitation amulet was just a pretty hunk of metal. It would be useless to anyone using it for magical means. I just hoped that no one had needed to use the amulet since my last visit.

I rested my hands on the wood framed, glass case and peeked over my shoulder. There was nothing to see but packets of dried herbs and boxes of tarot cards. I was alone, for now.

I turned my attention back to my task, ignoring the vampire bats that went into a feeding frenzy inside my stomach. I swallowed hard as I tested the latch that held the top of the case in place. Today was my lucky day. I wouldn't even have to put my lock picking skills to use. The case was unlocked.

I gently bit my lip and pulled the real amulet from my pocket. I lifted the glass lid higher, ready to use some quick sleight of hand to make the switch. Too bad my fingers were shaking like a vampire sucking blood in a Starbucks.

"Thank you, sweetie," a voice said from just over my shoulder. I jumped and the lid slammed shut on my wrist. *Son of a dung beetle.* I'd been caught red handed. In fact, my hand was rapidly shifting from red to purple. "They said you were coming."

I turned to see a tall woman made even taller by her blond hair which was styled into an epic beehive. My mouth dropped open and I gaped at her white cardigan, pink, high-necked dress, and platform sandals. She wasn't what I expected for a witch, though the face was all too familiar.

She was pointing at a murder of crows that were swarming outside the shop window, alighting on benches, trash bins, and lamp posts. Apparently, the crows were the ones who'd ratted me out. I scowled at the birds. *Traitors*. Crows had helped to lead me in the past, but this was the first time they'd betrayed me to an enemy. I looked from the window to the door, where more of the birds hovered. The door wasn't *that* far away...

"Oh, I wouldn't try it if I were you," a second woman said.

The short, round, dark haired woman, who'd appeared from nowhere, tilted her head to the side and narrowed her eyes at me from mere inches away. A tall, red haired woman went to the door and flipped the open sign to closed. My heart jumped into my throat at the click of the lock.

I had been considering running past the gauntlet of crows to make my escape. Too bad the witches could see right through me. And I was sure that they were witches. In fact, I knew with absolute certainty that these were the witches who owned the Cauldron and Noose. I'd know these women anywhere. Their faces had been invading my dreams for months.

I was locked inside with the witches from my dreams. This was truly a nightmare, and one I wasn't so sure I'd survive. My eyes flicked out the window, searching the street corner where I'd left Simon, but my backup was nowhere in sight. Had he run off when he saw that we were outnumbered? If he was off flirting with the wannabe pirate wench, I'd come back and haunt the heck out of him.

"So, um, I can explain," I said.

The three witches each raised a questioning brow in tandem, which was creepy and kind of impressive, but I never had a chance to finish. Simon, Cal, Emma, and London came bursting into the shop from the back storeroom. London was in wolf form, teeth bared.

"Might as well heat up the cauldron, Gretchen," the dark haired witch said. "Looks like we're having guests for lunch."

I swallowed hard and felt my skin pale. I so hope she didn't mean that the way it sounded.

Chapter 19

Thankfully, Evie (the blond), Gretchen (the red head), and Matilda (the brunette) didn't have plans to eat us for lunch. There would be no eating of humans so long as Cal managed to calm London. The weregirl was pacing the back room where the rest of us sat around a round table, drinking tea and eating finger sandwiches. Not, I was assured, sandwiches filled with fingers.

We would have looked like a normal bunch of friends if you pretended that London was a big dog and ignored the fact that my knees were knocking together under the table. Emma was already grilling Matilda for information on herb lore and tea mixtures while Simon flirted with Evie. Cal brought a plate of jerky over to London and, after doing the werewolf dominance dance, got her to sit and eat.

"So, are we all going to ignore the big, white, flying monkey in the room?" I asked.

My voice came out too loud and everyone's conversations cut off abruptly as they turned to stare at me. Even London raised her head from her plate. I cleared my throat and continued, hands bunched in my lap.

"Am I in trouble for borrowing your amulet?" I said. "If so, I'd like to discuss my punishment now, you know, before I pass out."

Beads of sweat rolled down my back, but I kept perfectly still. I held my breath waiting for the witches to reply.

"No, sweetie, you're not in trouble," Evie said.

"We've been waiting for you," Matilda said. "It's been a long time since we've had a death speaker for tea."

"A death speaker?" I asked.

"Yes, dear, a speaker for the dead," Gretchen said. "Mouth of the deceased. Dead man's guide. Call it what you will," she said with a wave of her hand.

"So you know about ghosts?" I asked.

"Of course, dear," Matilda said. "Spirit runs through all things. It is the spirit within plants that allows us to work our hedge magic, but only those born a death speaker can truly sense the spirits of the dead. You do communicate with ghosts, do you not?"

Cal moved closer and took my hand in his. He gave me a reassuring smile and squeezed my hand.

"Um, yeah, I can," I said. "We don't really speak exactly, it's not like I can hear their voices, but I help spirits of the dead with whatever unfinished business is chaining them here to our world. I...I help them into the light."

Saying I help spirits into the light always sounded cheesy to my ears, but the witches nodded sagely. No one laughed or rolled their eyes. Well, London may have tried, but she was still stuck in wolf form.

"You will be able to hear them eventually," Matilda said.

I swallowed hard and gripped Cal's hand tight. I wasn't so sure that I wanted the ability to hear ghosts. It was bad enough having to see and smell them.

"So she really is a death speaker?" Gretchen asked.

"Yes, I believe she is," Matilda said.

Gretchen and Evie smiled at each other and clapped their hands.

"Is it really that big of a deal?" I asked.

"It means we're doing our job," Evie said, eyes shining.

"Your job?" I asked, frowning.

"We make sure that the amulet is available to new death speakers," Gretchen said.

"But there hasn't been one for a long time," Evie said. "Matilda told us you'd come, but we were starting to think there wouldn't be a new death speaker during our lifetime."

"Wait, how did you make the amulet available?" Emma asked. "From what I remember, Yuki had to break in here and steal it. And that was after we researched everything we could find about Samhain and protections against ghosts."

"How do you think you found the amulet?" Matilda said with a wink. "We placed that trail of breadcrumbs online, leading any potential death speakers to our door."

"A door that was locked," Cal said.

My friends and I nodded, waiting for the witches to respond. It seemed ludicrous that these women were trying to take credit for the amulet falling into my hands. It's not like that had been easy.

"If it hadn't been for my impressive lock picking skills and legendary teaching ability, Yuki never would have made it into your shop or opened the case that housed the amulet," Simon said, studying his fingertips.

"Yes," Matilda said. "If we made things too easy, you wouldn't have believed the amulet was real."

Emma turned to me, brow lifted.

"She's right," she said.

"But what about the nightmares?" I asked, shaking my head. "If you wanted me to have the amulet, then why haunt my dreams?"

"That was my idea," Gretchen said, staring down into her tea.

"And it was a good idea," Matilda said, patting Gretchen's hand.

"We lost track of you," Evie said, blushing. "And we needed you to return the amulet after your first Samhain. You know, in case another death speaker turned up needing protection magic."

"So you terrorized my dreams to scare me into returning the amulet to your shop?" I asked.

"You scared her half to death," Emma said.

"Why didn't you just visit her dreams in a friendly way?" Cal asked. "Why resort to using fear and threats?"

The room filled with the smell of wet dog, overwhelming even the scent of salt brine that followed Sam's ghost. The pirates were still here of course. They sat on a pile of shipping crates, watching our discussion, and the werewolf eating from a china plate on the floor, with interest.

"We couldn't risk that Yuki wouldn't take the dreams seriously," Evie said. "Most people brush off happy dreams."

"You don't know Yuki very well then," Emma said. The witches turned to Emma, disbelieving looks on their faces. Emma shook her head and sighed. "The nightmares were totally unnecessary. Yuki's spirit animal visits her in her dreams all the time. It's not like she ignores it when her spirit guide tells her something without scaring her."

Actually, my spirit guide did a pretty good job of scaring the bejeezus out of me, but that was beside the point. Emma was right. If the witches had entered my dreams and explained why they needed the amulet back, I would have returned it. No mental anguish necessary.

Someone snorted behind me and I turned to see London wrapped in the blanket she'd been laying on moments before. *Um, hello, couldn't she put some clothes on?* The girl had shifted back to her human form and managed to sneer at me while standing there practically naked.

"Give the ladies a break, Yuki," she said. "The dreams would have frightened you no matter what they said or how they said it. You're scared of everything, even bridges."

I ground my teeth and clenched my fists in my lap—it was that or strangle the girl. In fact, I probably ought to sit on my hands before I did something I'd later regret. I'd had it with London's rude comments.

Today could not end soon enough. We still had a lengthy car ride to Cape Cod ahead of us and I was pretty sure we'd be crossing some bridges on the way. With London along for the ride, it was going to be a hellishly long trip.

Chapter 20

I left the Cauldron and Noose with a promise to return soon. Matilda, Gretchen, and Evie still weren't on my Christmas card list, but they knew a lot more about this death speaker stuff than I did. I hoped to learn more from them about people like me who could communicate with the dead. You didn't have to be psychic to see more trips to Salem in my near future.

I just hoped future trips didn't involve a car full of people. Emma was driving and Simon had called shotgun before we even left the occult shop, which meant I was in the back seat again with Cal and London. As the tiniest person in the car, I was seated in the middle. That meant I was way closer to the weregirl than I was comfortable with, especially since London growled whenever my boots crossed over toward her side of the car.

Maybe next time, Cal could drive me down in his truck. I wanted him to be there as I learned more about my psychic gift. Cal and I had to keep parts of our lives secret from so many people, it made me want to share everything with him all the more.

"It's incredible finally discovering there are other people out there with your talents," Cal said.

It was like he'd plucked the thought from my brain. Who knows, maybe he did. My ankle tingled, reminding me that Cal and I had a pretty intense connection. Although our spirit tattoos weren't the only intense thing between us.

I looked up into Cal's tanned face and I felt dizzy, as if I could fall into Cal's deep, blue eyes. Instead, I ran my hands through his hair and pulled him close.

"Yeah, it's nice knowing I'm not alone," I said.

"You were never alone," he said, lips brushing my ear as we held each other close. "You will never, ever be alone."

"Will you two stop whispering?" London said. "You're giving me a headache."

I sighed, closed my eyes, and leaned my head on Cal's shoulder.

"Are you sure we can't leave her at a rest stop somewhere?" I asked. "We could pick her up on the way back to Maine." *Maybe.*

Cal kissed my forehead and smiled.

"Sorry, but no," he said. "And for the record, her hearing is really sensitive right now."

Right, London was dealing with sensitive hearing due to her frequent shifting, hence the headache. Oh, and she probably heard everything I just said. *Oops.*

I lifted my head and glanced at London. She was sitting with her forehead resting on the cool window glass. Sweat was beaded on her neck and heat came off her in waves. Was she close to shifting again? I was pretty sure I didn't want to be crammed into the back seat with a wolf who obviously hated my guts.

I poked Cal in the ribs to get his attention and tried to think of some way to distract London. Maybe if I could keep her human mind busy, her wolf would get bored and take a nap.

"So, um, have you been to Cape Cod before?" I asked.

London shrugged.

"Of course," she said. "My parents brought my sister and me here as kids. Haven't you been before?"

"No," I said. "My parents don't get a lot of time off, so we never traveled this far."

"It's not like it's *that* far," she said condescendingly.

"I've never been either," Cal said.

"You've been to one coastal town, you've seen them all," Simon piped in.

"Whatever," London said.

She crossed her arms and went back to staring out the window, but the heat coming off her skin had subsided. I hoped it stayed that way. I really didn't want to have to talk to her anymore. London was about as friendly as a vampire with a toothache.

I caught Emma's glance in the rearview mirror and she rolled her eyes. I wasn't the only one who found London's personality grating. Thankfully, London stayed quiet until we neared Cape Cod. Unfortunately, the first words out of her mouth almost gave me a heart attack.

"Look, Yuki, Sagamore Bridge," she said, pointing straight ahead.

I checked my face, and Cal's shoulder, for drool—I hadn't been sleeping well lately and managed to doze off after we skirted south of Boston—and frowned.

"Very funny, London," I grumped.

"Um, Yuki," Emma said. "She's not joking."

I rubbed my face and blinked out the windshield. *Son of a dung beetle.* The biggest bridge I'd ever seen, even bigger than the Piscataqua River Bridge, loomed ahead of us like the skeleton of a slumbering beast.

"Can't we go around it?" I asked, pulling out my phone. There had to be another way out to the Cape.

"Sorry, love," Simon said. "It's the Sagamore or the Bourne, and the Sagamore Bridge is closest."

I glared at our navigator, but soon turned my scowl to the girl sitting beside me. London had a smug look on her face and I realized that she'd awoken me on purpose. If I'd stayed sleeping a few minutes longer, I'd have been unconscious for the terrifying trip over the Sagamore.

Cal was also coming to the same conclusion. He entwined his fingers with mine and gave my hand a squeeze as the car filled with the scent of wet dog. I looked up into his face to see his wolf pacing just behind his eyes.

Cal turned to stare over my head at London. His nostrils flared and he bared his teeth. His hand felt impossibly warm where we touched. For the second time today, I worried about being in tight quarters with a wolf.

Cal may have spent many years as a pacifist, but he was now the werewolf pack alpha—and London had crossed the line. Cal was protective of his pack, especially of me. If London continued behaving like a threat, he had the power to make her life miserable. But as much as the idea of London cleaning the latrines at Wolf Camp made me all warm and fuzzy inside, I knew that with a car full of angry werewolves things could get out of hand fast.

"Um, Cal?" I asked. "A little help here? Th-th-that bridge is coming up pretty quick."

Cal's wolf retreated and concern bled into his eyes as he looked down into my pale face. He pulled me to him, my face buried in his chest as the car began its trip across the expanse of concrete and metal. I took a deep breath, the smell of sunshine and pine needles filling my head and pushed thoughts of ghosts and bridges away. He stroked my hair and murmured something comforting as Emma continued to make her way toward Cape Cod.

"It's safe now, Yuki," Emma said. "You can open your eyes."

"Thanks," I mumbled into Cal's chest. His muscular arms were still wrapped around me and I didn't really want to pull away, but the smell of salt brine, burning meat, gunpowder, and rum were growing stronger. The ghosts were getting restless, which meant we were definitely on the right track.

I lifted my head and winced. I squinted against the afternoon sun that poured into the car and took in our new surroundings. According to a road sign, we were on Route 6 heading down the Cape toward Provincetown. We wouldn't be going that far though. Our final destination was Wellfleet after a stop in Eastham.

On a positive note, there were no large bridges in sight. I let out a huge breath, a slow smile building on my lips. We were nearly there.

As we approached Eastham, Emma stayed on Route 6, passing signs for Bridge Road. Good idea. I didn't think my heart could take another bridge right now. If we couldn't find Bellamy's treasure along Route 6, we could take the alternate road later.

I turned my attention from the white summer homes and scenic vistas to check the notes Emma and I had made regarding The Devil's Cliff, Lucifer Land. Though Sam had been known to spend his time at a drinking hole in Eastham, and had reputedly met Mary Hallett beneath an apple tree across the street from an Eastham inn, our best guess for Lucifer Land was an area near the Marconi Station in Wellfleet.

"So should we stop in Eastham first, or carry on to Wellfleet?" I asked.

"I still think Wellfleet is our best shot," Emma said. "We can start there and work our way back up the Cape if the sea cliffs don't pan out."

I waited to see if our ghost pirates had anything to add, but aside from the smell, they didn't make an appearance. Did they ride along on the roof or something? The thought of ghost pirates surfing on the top of Emma's car while we drove down the Cape was ridiculous. For the first time today, I laughed.

Maybe this trip would work out after all.

Chapter 21

I knew the instant we'd crossed into Wellfleet, since some civic-minded person had filled a small, white row boat with potting soil and turned it into a flower garden set into the road median. Painted along the side of the boat in black paint were the words, "Welcome to Wellfleet."

I expected an ominous chill or the rattle of chains or maybe even a rousting round of Yo Ho Ho and a Bottle of Rum!, but aside from the odd use of a boat for a flower pot, Wellfleet looked much like other towns along the New England seacoast. Since this was my first time helping ghost pirates search for missing treasure, I couldn't help but be disappointed.

Emma pulled into a small filling station to get gas and we all got out of the car to stretch our legs. I couldn't resist searching the roof of the car for pirates, but the ghosts were nowhere in sight. I turned to ask Cal if he wanted to go grab snacks and my jaw dropped all the way to my paint spattered boots.

London took Cal's hand and tugged him toward the small convenience store like a tethered balloon. Cal looked poleaxed, but followed, mumbling an apology and a promise to bring snacks for everyone.

I shook my head and reigned in the desire to stomp my feet. If I never saw London again, it would be too soon. I knew the girl was dealing with a lot and that with her parents out of town Cal and Simon were her only real support system while she dealt with the onset of werewolf maturity, but she needed to learn some boundaries. Pawing all over another girl's boyfriend was not cool.

And it's not like she had to lean on someone to walk the short distance to the convenience store. Due to her werewolf metabolism, London's ankle had already healed; her recent shift into wolf form had taken care of that.

"Should we ask someone inside for directions to The Devil's Cliff, Lucifer Land?" Emma asked, wiping her hands with a paper towel.

"I'll go charm the locals," Simon said with a wink. "You girls stay here and watch the car."

Emma certainly wasn't watching the car. Her eyes followed Simon as he swaggered across the street to where a small group of ladies sat at a café table. Soon the women were blushing and fanning themselves. More than one woman scribbled something onto a napkin and gave it to Simon. That guy really was a piece of work.

"There is something seriously wrong with this picture," I said.

Emma raised an eyebrow and leaned back against her car.

"What do you mean?" she asked.

"My boyfriend is inside being groped by a smoking hot weregirl and your boyfriend is across the street getting the phone numbers of every woman in Wellfleet," I said.

Emma laughed and shook her head.

"That's not what I see," she said. "I see Cal, the most patient guy on the planet, putting up with the most annoying member of his pack in order to help her through the change."

"And Simon?" I asked.

"Simon is a flirt," she said, shrugging. "But he's actually just getting directions."

It was true. Simon returned with a hastily drawn map of a nearby cliff walk. The locals pointed out a place called the Devil's Pasture to the south in Eastham, a place called White Cedar Swamp where the "Witch of Wellfleet" was rumored to have lived, and a stretch of cliffs known as Lucifer's Leap near Marconi beach.

"It must be this cliff walk, Lucifer's Leap," I said.

"Aye, we'll try there first," Simon said, sliding an arm around Emma's waist.

He kissed my friend deeply and I swore I could hear the sighing from our disappointed audience across the street. These days Simon made his affection for Emma known. He may be a flirt, but his heart was taken—much to the chagrin of the ladies of Eastham.

I turned away and caught sight of London licking a lollipop and batting her eyelashes at my boyfriend. Cal ignored London and headed my way, arms laden with snacks. I tried to smile, but I'm pretty sure it came out as a grimace. The suggestive way that London ate her candy while giving Cal puppy dog eyes made my blood boil.

I spun around, not wanting to look at London for another second, and stopped dead. Sam and his pirate buddies were examining the nozzle from one of the gas pumps with serious faces. As I watched, one of the Grays drew a pistol from its holster and held it up to the nozzle. The others started nodding, gesturing to their own weapons.

Ah, the ghosts thought the gas pumps were some weird, new-fangled gun. I shook my head and opened the door to the backseat.

"Come on guys," I said. "No time for playing with toys. We have treasure to find."

Sam straightened and waved his men forward. When they reached the car, they climbed onto the roof and sat like they were riding on top of a horse drawn carriage. Ha! I knew it. They did hitch a ride up there.

Everyone else got inside and buckled up, Cal distributing snacks. He'd grabbed me a box of trail mix and a bag of Skittles, my favorite. I smiled and kissed him on the cheek.

Cal grinned and relaxed into the seat beside me. I felt bad for getting so jealous over London. It wasn't like her behavior was Cal's fault. I shared my Skittles with Cal and he tossed them into his mouth then leaned in for a kiss. The flavor explosion, and the feeling of Cal's fingers trailing up my neck and across my earlobe, left me tingling all over.

A loud crunch came from behind me as London bit down on her lollipop and I smiled against Cal's lips. It didn't matter how hard London tried, Cal was mine. I felt the engine roar as Emma pulled out into traffic. We headed toward Lucifer's Leap; me, Emma, three werewolves, and a gaggle of hitchhiking ghosts.

Chapter 22

The drive to Marconi Beach, part of the Massachusetts National Seashore, was scenic, but I was too keyed up for playing tourist. Simon spouted off facts about the beach, and the Marconi Station site to the north, ad nauseam. I learned that an inventor name Marconi, like I couldn't have guessed that was his name, had made the first transatlantic wireless communication between the U.S. and England from this spot back in 1903.

Historic scientific breakthroughs might have interested me under different circumstances, but today I was more interested in Cape Cod's earlier history. The waters here were known as the "Graveyard of the Atlantic" or the "ocean graveyard" due to the fact that over 3,000 ships had wrecked off this coastline. The *Whydah*, Sam Bellamy's pirate galley, had gone down here while he was trying to return to Cape Cod to be reunited with his true love, Mary Hallett.

Had the sinking of the *Whydah* been due to dangerous waters, or the curse? It seemed like more than coincidence that the pirate ship went down less than a month after Bellamy was cursed by a man intent on joining his crew. But then again, this was the Graveyard of the Atlantic.

We'd made it to Marconi Beach and I stood watching the waves crash against the sandy beach to the east of the walking trail. It felt desolate up here with only the cry of gulls and the whispering of sea grass rustling in the breeze. How many other ghosts wandered these shores? I shivered, pulling my eyes from the ocean graveyard, and continued my walk along the sandy path.

Sand cliffs reached high above Marconi Beach. I could easily imagine Mary Hallett here. A young girl, cast out, cursed to walk alone atop these cliffs, keeping a watchful eye on the sea for her beloved. The sail of every ship on the horizon would have lifted her hopes, only to dash them on the rocks below. We followed in Mary's footsteps, climbing over the cliffs of Lucifer's Leap, but there was no sign of treasure.

I caught Sam's mournful eyes tracing the location of his sunken ship, and watery grave. It would make more sense for Sam's "dearest treasure" to be out there beneath the waves and shifting sand, but he shook his head when I suggested his treasure was beyond our reach. He'd looked away and continued pacing the cliffs.

At five o'clock, we called it quits and headed back to Emma's car. After a brief discussion, we decided to explore nearby White Cedar Swamp. The trailhead was at the Marconi Station to the north and we picked a route to the station that took us through the town of Wellfleet. Sam looked disappointed as we piled back into the car, pirates riding on top, and my stomach twisted.

Was it only wishful thinking to believe that we'd be able to locate Sam's treasure and send his ghost into the light? I hoped we'd have better luck in the swamp where the Witch of Wellfleet was reputed to wander.

But that was assuming that the legendary Witch of Wellfleet was Sam's lost love, Mary Hallett. The townspeople of Eastham had tortured and imprisoned Mary, calling her a witch and casting her out to be exiled to the swamps and beaches of nearby Wellfleet. Did that mean that Mary Hallett and the Witch of Wellfleet were one and the same? It was hard to untangle the web of truth and hearsay.

"I'm in dire need of sustenance," Simon said, interrupting my gloomy thoughts. "And if I don't cross paths with a cup of coffee soon, I may die of exhaustion."

"I second that," Emma said.

"Wimps," I said, smiling. "Didn't you get any sleep last night?"

"No," they said in unison.

Simon winked and Emma blushed. *Oh, ew.*

"Anyway," I said, rolling my eyes. "How about we vote? Who wants to stop for coffee?"

Everyone raised their hand in favor of food and caffeine. Well, everyone who was living. The ghosts probably would have argued for mugs of rum, but, thankfully, they didn't get a vote.

We were in luck. A convenience store on the way back into Wellfleet had coffee and microwavable veggie burritos. I was in take-out bliss until Sam and his crew sidled over to the picnic table I was sitting on. For the record, stinky ghost pirates do not go with guacamole. I sighed and pitched the rest of my burrito in the trash.

"Ghosts?" Cal asked.

He reached out and smoothed my hair behind my ear, leaving tingles where his fingers brushed my cheek.

"Yeah," I said, giving him a rueful smile. "They're a great way to diet."

He shook his head, brow wrinkled.

"I wish there was some way to protect you from all this," he said. "If there was something I could do to help, I'd do it in a second. Anything at all."

"I know," I said. "It helps just knowing that."

"But it doesn't help you eat," he said, frowning.

"No, but I'll be done with these guys soon enough," I said. "And who knows, maybe the gals at the Cauldron and Noose can give me some tips on tuning out the ghosts. Maybe there's even a way to keep them at a distance. That would be convenient, you know, for meal times."

"I can think of other times it would be convenient," he said. Cal leaned in, lips brushing mine. "It'd be nice to know we didn't have an audience."

Cal had a point. A few of The Grays were leering at us from across the parking lot. Cal tipped my head back and I forgot all about our ghostly eavesdroppers. My lips parted and the convenience store parking lot disappeared. All that existed in that moment was Cal's strong arms around me and his lips on mine.

"Now I've lost *my* appetite," London said.

I broke away from Cal and sighed. *Thanks a lot London, way to ruin the mood.*

"I guess we should be on our way," Cal said. "We have a lot of ground to cover before dark."

The smell of salt brine filled my head and I knew without turning around that Sam was standing close, watching me with sad, blue eyes the color of the ocean waters that had swallowed him. I shook my head, trying to push away thoughts of the pirate's tragic death. Cal was right, it was time to go.

Chapter 23

I had hoped that White Cedar Swamp would turn up clues to Sam's treasure. Too bad the swamp trails didn't produce anything more than ticks and mosquito bites.

"If I wanted bug bites, I'd have stayed at Wolf Camp," London grumbled. "This is a total waste of time."

I had to admit, she had a point. We'd walked the entire trail system, even having Cal and Simon roam ahead in wolf form, with nothing to show for our efforts except itchy, red welts and an irritated ghost pirate.

Sam was waving his hands in agitation and pointing toward the car. *Yeah, yeah, we get the message.*

"Okay," I said, nodding. "Maybe we'll have better luck at Devil's Pasture."

Eyes on my smelly spectral companions, I strode toward the car—and off the boarded trail. The earth fell away as my boots slid beneath muddy water. Belatedly, I remembered that ghosts can float on thin air. Too bad humans like me need solid ground beneath our feet.

I barely had time to yelp before my head sunk under filthy swamp water. I struggled to kick my way up to the surface, but all I managed to do was churn more mud into the murky water. I fought to stay calm, but I couldn't see and my lungs were burning against the strain of holding my breath.

I'd always feared death by fire, believing that burning at the stake would be the most painful way to die—a fear made all the worse by the J-team's threats and taunts—but I was beginning to think that the pain of drowning was a close second. If I didn't reach the surface soon, my head was going to explode. I flailed my arms in an attempt to swim and my hand hit something moving through the water. Whatever it was, it was bigger than a fish. *Oh em gees,* were there alligators in Massachusetts?

Something locked onto my arm and wrapped itself around my waist. I would have screamed if there'd been any air left in my lungs. I figured the creature that had grabbed me was going to drag me down and eat me, but instead my head broke through the surface of the water. I gasped for breath, but no sooner than my lungs filled, the air was knocked out of them again as I was tossed onto the leaf strewn embankment. My eyes fluttered open to see London leaning over me.

London, who I thought hated my guts, had just saved my life. I didn't think I could be more surprised—I was wrong. Eyes flashing, London leaned in close, her hair dripping swamp water onto my face. That look froze me in place, my body unmoving as she struggled with some unknown emotion. London hovered above me, her arms shaking, the tips of her ears turning furry and poking up through the strands of her pixie haircut. I blinked in confusion. Had she saved me only to grow fur and teeth and bite me?

With a growl, London dove in close to hiss into my ear. Even covered in cool swamp water, her skin was hot and feverish and warm spittle flew from her mouth to speckle the side of my face.

"Foolish, clumsy human," she said tightly. Her fingers dug painfully into my shoulders and I flinched. My reaction drew her lips away from her teeth, which were already elongating into fangs—fangs that were only an inch from my jugular. "So weak. You're not worthy of our alpha. You don't belong in our pack. Stay away from Cal or I'll put you down, permanently. He's MINE."

"Yuki!" Cal yelled.

London rolled off me, quickly loping off into the trees, and was suddenly replaced by Cal. His strong arms wrapped around me, holding me tightly to his chest where his heart seemed to beat so slowly compared to my own. He whispered how much he loved me and that everything was alright, but even Cal's steadying presence couldn't stop the dizzying questions that whirled around my brain.

Cal's warm, dry hands lifted me upright, while still wrapped in his arms, and he murmured thanks to every conceivable god while Simon spouted off a litany of curses for foolish girls who don't look where they're walking. Even Emma rushed up to add her comments about bacterial counts in swamp water, but I could barely hear their voices over the storm of confusion in my head. It was like someone had filled my skull with a hive of industrious worker bees and they were all buzzing about the same thing—London had threatened to kill me.

Chapter 24

I wiped at my muddy clothes, flakes of drying mud fluttering to the ground like dying bats in their death throes. I crouched down and checked my appearance in the side mirror of Emma's car and grimaced. I looked like something from a creature double feature.

"Ugh," I said. "I'm glad we just have one stop left at the Devil's Pasture. I need a bath and a gallon of shower gel."

At the mention of Devil's Pasture, Sam and his crew moved closer. Their multitude of scents was a relief from the reek of old mud, frog poop, and rotting vegetation. I gave Sam a wry grin. You know you smell bad when the ghosts who are haunting you smell better than you do.

"Here," Cal said, handing me another towel.

He'd laid beach towels and blankets from the trunk over Emma's back seat in an effort to keep me from ruining my friend's upholstery, but kept a few towels in reserve for me to mop off with. I smiled gratefully and wiped over my face with shaking hands.

I hadn't stopped shaking since the incident with London. Everyone thought it was because of my accidental fall into the swamp—everyone except me and London, who was now watching my every move. I could feel her green eyes carve their way through my flesh, even as I turned away.

I needed to tell Cal about what had happened with London, but I couldn't do it here, not yet. Simon and London had incredible werewolf hearing and Emma was eyeing me like something in a specimen jar.

"Did you swallow any swamp water?" Emma asked.

"No, why?" I asked.

"Are you sure?" Cal asked. "It looked like London had to give you mouth to mouth."

I coughed, eyes bulging at the comment. The memory of London's spittle hot against my cheek knocked the last of the air from my lungs. The unstable werewolf had leant in close enough to give me mouth to mouth, but she wasn't trying to save my life. She'd used the opportunity to threaten me away from Cal, though I was still unsure why she'd dragged me from the water in the first place. Maybe it was to earn brownie points with Cal and Simon before she got me out of the picture.

Emma just took my coughing fit as proof that I'd swallowed something nasty.

"You need to take something for that cough," she said, rummaging through her medical kit.

Emma wanted to stop somewhere for hot water to make one of her herbal healing teas, but settled for watching me take a huge dose of a bitter tasting herbal tincture. The stuff made me feel queasy, joining the chaotic party that vampire bats were currently having in my stomach.

My discomfort increased when London loped over and launched herself into the car. I did not want to have to sit next to her on the way to Eastham. Fortunately, Cal gave me an excuse to sit by the door.

"Ready?" he asked. "We're running out of daylight. We should go check out the Devils' Pasture."

"Okay, let's get this over with," I said.

I started to duck my head inside the car, but Cal put a hand to my shoulder and smiled.

"Actually, do you mind sitting by the open window?" he asked.

"Oh my God, I really do smell like frog poop, don't I?" I asked.

"Um, no?" he asked. I could feel my eyebrows rise to my hairline and Cal rubbed the back of his neck. "Well, yeah. It's kind of strong."

Right, werewolf senses. The pack could probably smell me all the way in Maine. I shrugged and stood back, waiting for Cal to slide in beside London. Just an hour ago their close proximity would have made me jealous, but not now. Now it just frightened me half to death.

We drove to Eastham in silence. My friends were trying not to breathe in the swamp funk from my accidental dip in the Marconi swamp and I was too preoccupied over London's threats to strike up a conversation. I tried to figure out what her angry words had meant, if anything. It was all so confusing, but I did have a theory.

London had been touchy feely with Cal and Simon from the beginning and now I had to wonder if she'd been vying for a spot at the top of the pack all along. Her claim on Cal didn't seem to come from any feelings for him or any reciprocating behavior on his part. London just didn't appear to like her position at the bottom of the pack hierarchy, and it looked like she was prepared to do whatever it took to claw her way to the top.

I pulled at my mud stiffened clothes, a growing tightness in my throat. I guess it made sense that London had picked me to dominate in her rise to power. As a human, and one who wasn't physically strong, I was perceived as the weakest pack member. If she knew about my abduction this past spring, then she probably assumed I was vulnerable to bullying. I had worked through the fear and anxiety that had paralyzed me after my abduction, but I was still healing. Leave it to London to tear off the scabs from my old wounds.

I stole a glance past Cal to where London sat looking out the window. As if she could sense my attention, she turned cold eyes my way and flashed me a vicious grin. I swallowed hard and clutched my stomach.

"Are you okay?" Cal asked, brow wrinkling.

I took a deep breath and shook my head.

"Not really," I said. "Can we stop somewhere? I don't feel so good."

"Sure, hang on," he said. Cal, rubbing my back, turned to face Emma in the driver's seat. "We need to find a place to pull over. Yuki's feeling sick."

"I knew you swallowed some of that swamp water," Emma said, watching me in the rearview mirror.

"I doubt it's the water that's made her sick, Love," Simon said. "Your herbal tonics may be effective, but they taste like something that rolled in pine pitch and died."

I rested my head on Cal's shoulder and moaned.

"I don't think talking about the taste of dead things is helping," Cal said.

"Poor Yuki," London said. "It must be hard being such a weak human."

My fingernails dug into my palm, but I stifled the urge to reach across the car and slap London's satisfied grin off from her face. The weregirl was enjoying her game of cat and mouse. Little did she know, this mouse could roar.

*****

I was going to expose London's little game, but first I had to throw up. Whether from stress, a ghost induced migraine, or Emma's tincture, my stomach was roiling like a ship in a windstorm. My muddy boots hit the gravel the second Emma brought the car to a stop.

She'd pulled into a small, one pump gas station that advertized restrooms with a sign that pointed around back. I dashed behind the station and into one of the dark stalls, barely taking the time to close the door behind me. Tincture, tea, and veggie burrito came up in a noxious mix and I flushed the toilet. I stood there shaking, waiting to see if my stomach was finished heaving, when I heard someone enter the restrooms.

"Emma?" I asked.

Maybe my medically minded friend had come to see how the patient was doing. Usually, I avoided all the fuss, but I would have liked the opportunity to share with Emma what really had happened back at the swamp.

I waited, listening for a reply over my own shaky breaths. I thought I heard footsteps, but no one answered and there were no sounds of water running or stall doors opening and closing. The only thing I could sense was the increasing salt brine scent of an agitated ghost. I just hoped that the Prince of Pirates stayed outside the restroom door. There was something slimy about a ghost guy flitting about the girl's bathrooms, even if he had been dead for three hundred years.

I shook my head, turned to unlatch the door, and stepped out into the larger room. I lurched toward the sinks and gasped. Someone had written, "DON'T TELL" in large, dark red letters across one of the mirrors.

Clenching my fists, I forced myself forward for a closer look. The letters were scrawled in lipstick, not blood, but the message was menacing just the same. I assumed that London was covering her bases and making sure that I didn't spill about her earlier threats. The funny thing was, her attempt to scare me hadn't worked. The garish display didn't make me want to run and hide. It just made me mad as hell.

I laughed and bared my teeth at my reflection. I'd been the victim of bullies before, but never had anyone tried to force their way into my relationship with Cal. The thought of giving him up, the love of my life, because someone wanted to use his status to gain power was preposterous. I'd never let fear come between us.

In fact, if Cal knew what London was up to, he'd be the first to put a stop to it. But I didn't want to rely on my friends to fix this. I rinsed my mouth out with tap water and nodded at the grim face in the mirror. It was time to confront my new nemesis.

Chapter 25

I set my jaw, hands fisted at my sides, and strode toward London where she leaned against the car beside Cal. She narrowed her eyes at me, but I continued forward, boots crunching against the gravel. Cal's head tilted to the side, his blue eyes searching my face. I studied him for just a moment, barely the length of a breath, but long enough to see the love and concern in his handsome face and the set of his muscular shoulders.

I flashed him a smile to let him know everything was okay, and then felt the line of my lips harden as I turned my attention to London. The weregirl tensed and drew herself up to her full height. The way her eyes followed me was menacing, but I wasn't going to back down. Cal was worth fighting for.

I stopped inches away from London's face, the toes of my boots scraping against her sandals. London's nostrils flared and she offered a tight smile that didn't reach her eyes.

"Why, Yuki, you look terrible," she said. "Maybe you should go lie down."

"I'm sure you'd like me to go away, London," I said. "But that's not going to happen."

She waved her hand dismissively and rolled her eyes.

"Why would I care what you do?" she said. "You mean nothing to me."

"If I mean nothing, then why did you threaten me?" I asked.

I could feel Cal tense beside us while Emma and Simon pressed forward, suddenly interested in what was going on between me and London. I raised a hand to Cal, letting him know this was my battle, not his.

"So what if I did?" London asked, shrugging. "What are you going to do about it?"

"I challenge you to a duel," I said.

"You'd never beat me in combat," she said.

I wasn't a fighter, and facing down an angry werewolf was potential suicide, but the thing was, I knew I wouldn't have to face London in combat. I'd been listening all those nights that Cal pored over pack law. In fact, while my friends were setting up the new pack database, I read through every page of notes that they'd accumulated in their research. So I knew that the person who'd been threatened first—which in this case was me—got to choose the type of duel, and I knew exactly what to pick.

"Yes, but I never said this was a physical duel," I said. "I challenge you to a duel of wits."

"Well, you don't get to pick," she sneered. London leaned in close and licked her lips. "You laid down the challenge, so I get to choose the type of duel and I want hand-to-hand combat."

"I made the challenge, but I wasn't the first the lay down a threat," I said.

"And what kind of proof do you have?" she asked. "This supposed threat is just your word against mine."

"Actually, I do have proof," I said, holding up my phone. "I snapped a picture of the message you left on the bathroom mirrors, and I'm sure if you dumped out your purse I'd find the same lipstick you wrote it with."

London blanched, her hands tightening around her purse. I'd outsmarted the hotheaded weregirl and she knew it. My friends pressed in close, wondering what this was all about, but letting me have my say.

"Fine, whatever," she said. "Go ahead and pick your silly duel."

"I choose a trivia battle," I said. "Pitting your knowledge against mine."

"Seriously?" she asked. "I'll still beat you. You might as well give up now, Yuki."

"If I may interject," Simon said. "You don't know your adversary very well, if you think Yuki will give up. She's an incredibly stubborn human."

"I'm especially stubborn when someone threatens me to stay away from my boyfriend," I said. "Cal and I are soul mates. Death threats won't keep us apart."

"Death threats?" Cal said, stepping between us. "Yuki, if I'd known..."

"I know," I said, reaching up to touch his face. "You'd do anything to protect me, and I love you for that, but some battles I have to fight on my own. If I don't do this, then what's to stop every new upstart werewolf from doing exactly what London's doing now?"

"I won't let a member of my pack harm you," he said.

"It won't come to that," I said. "I proposed a duel of wits, remember?"

"Subject?" Simon asked, raising an eyebrow.

"Anime trivia," I said, letting a slow smile slide across my face.

Emma leaned forward and bumped knuckles as she whispered in my ear, "Girl, you so have this."

"I know," I said. "But we'll have to wait until we get back to the beach house to settle this. Gordy will have to be our Alex Trebek."

"Do you accept this challenge?" Simon asked, turning his attention to London.

"I...I don't..." London said.

"Yes," Cal said, looking fierce. "Yes, she does."

"Um, yes," she said, staring at her shoes.

The word of the pack alpha was final. London and I were going to have an anime trivia duel. I couldn't wait to whoop her butt. Too bad we had to finish our business with the ghost pirates first.

"Good, now let's stop fighting so we can help Sam find his treasure," I said.

I stomped toward the car, Cal at my back and Emma hurrying to my side.

"Her plan backfired you know," Emma whispered. I knew that the werewolves could probably hear us, but I didn't care. I just smiled and kept walking. "He loves you all the more for standing up to London and for fighting for him."

"It would be impossible to love Yuki any more than I already do," Cal said, walking up behind me. "Our love is all consuming. But I'm happy she thought I was worth fighting for."

I turned to look into Cal's blue eyes, a myriad of emotions flickering beneath their surface. His hands twitched as he held himself rigid. Knowing Cal, he still felt responsible for London's threats. At least he was happy with the way I'd handled things on my own. I stepped into his arms and laced my fingers in his hair.

"I will always fight for you," I said. I pulled myself up on tiptoe and brushed my lips against his. "I love you Calvin Miller. Don't you forget it."

Cal's strong arms crushed me to his chest and his soft lips gliding across mine seemed to search my mouth for answers. I pulled him closer, letting him know with my every movement just how much he meant to me. London and her power play faded away, and there was only me and Cal and the dizzying effects of our kiss.

Chapter 26

"So this is the Devil's Pasture," Simon said. "I expected something more...impressive."

Emma had driven up the Cape to an overgrown field in Eastham after following the dubious directions of the young guy working back at the gas station. The station attendant claimed the pasture was the site of devil worship and ghost hauntings, though I was pretty sure his only exposure to demons and ghosts was playing video games. His information didn't seem all that reliable and I wondered if we'd ever find Sam's pirate booty. This place looked more likely to turn up ticks than treasure.

"Are you sure this is the place?" I asked, turning in a circle. "It's just grass and trees."

Well, grass, trees, and ragweed. I had to pinch my nose to stifle a sneeze. The field was covered in the evil, yellow blossoms. Maybe that's why it was called the Devil's Pasture. The place tormented allergy sufferers with its malevolent cloud of pollen that hung in the air like a vile miasma. If weeds could twirl their mustachios, I'm sure these plants certainly would.

"Didn't you see the cemetery up the road?" Emma asked. "The attendant agreed with what the locals told me when I asked earlier up in Wellfleet. They said to turn up the first dirt track, just past the Eastham Cove Burying Ground. This has to be the right place."

I'd gone past an old cemetery without noticing? I really was preoccupied. I blinked at my friends and shook my head.

"Guess I was distracted by the stench of eau du swamp," I said.

"As were we all," Simon said, pulling a face.

Actually, I'd been absorbed in my own thoughts, ruminating over the confrontation with London and reflecting on Cal's kiss which lingered like tiny sparks of electricity on my lips. But now that we were here, it was time to focus on my ghost problem and help Sam with his final wishes.

"Okay, well if this is the Devil's Pasture, the treasure must be around here somewhere," I said.

I held my head high and strode forward, trying to sound more confident than I felt. If I couldn't find Sam's treasure, he'd stay trapped here in our world where he'd likely haunt me forever. That was one outcome I seriously wanted to avoid. Plus, I really wanted to help him somehow. It would be nice to see the handsome pirate smile for once. Since the moment he popped into my life, his face had been a roadmap of despair. I prayed that this wouldn't be just another dead end.

My friends spread out, pushing through the tall weeds, scenting the air, and kicking at the ground. At Emma's startled intake of breath, I rushed over to see what she'd found. But with one glance, I could see it wasn't treasure. Not unless Sam's treasure slithered.

Emma bent down and held her hand out to a snake that glided toward her through the grass. After a brief moment of introductions, Emma began nodding her head and asking questions. The snake took off toward the back of the field where the grass met the tree line and Emma hurried after it.

"Does the snake know where the treasure is?" I asked.

It wasn't a silly question. Emma's spirit animal was a serpent which gave her the uncanny ability to speak to any snake she encountered. She still wasn't comfortable with her new talent, but apparently she'd set aside her unease to ask the snake some questions. Emma's shoulders tensed, but she kept her eyes on the grass.

"She said there's something old buried back here," she said, shrugging. "I don't know if it's pirate treasure or not, but it's worth checking out."

I lifted a hand to my face to ward off a wave of dizziness as my head filled with the scent of ghost pirates. Sam was suddenly hovering at my shoulder, The Grays at his back. I tried to ignore the fluttering in my stomach and followed Emma and the snake.

At the edge of the field was a cluster of vine covered stones. I held my breath and leaned in to take a closer look, hoping there was something here. I jerked a handful of overgrown weeds back away from the flat surface of a rock and gasped.

A name was etched there beneath layers of moss and centuries of dirt. I stumbled back, hand shaking. This wasn't the treasure I'd been expecting, but I knew we'd found what was most precious to Sam Bellamy.

"Yuki, are you okay?" Cal asked, reaching out to steady me.

Suddenly Sam and the other pirates were pressing in close, circling the stone and giving me a killer headache with their dizzying combination of smells. But a new smell had joined the ghostly scents. A young girl stood by one of the stones, her long, blond hair shining golden in the waning light—and she smelled of apple blossoms.

We'd found Sam's true love, Mary Hallett.

I thought back on the wording of Sam's request, the unfinished business that tied him to this world. He'd wanted me to bring the ring from his body to the site of his most precious treasure. If I'd thought more about his relationship with Mary and the tragic end to their romance, I might have guessed what he truly wanted. But I'd been too caught up in the idea of buried treasure, distracted by who the man had been in life and not paying attention to the reason that drove him to a life of piracy in the first place.

Sam had sailed away from Cape Cod in hopes of earning the fortune required to marry his true love. When he achieved that goal, after two years of piracy, he set course for Mary Hallett. On this final voyage, he carried with him a beautiful ring—a ring that held an eternal promise.

I reached into my messenger bag, having to try twice to unzip the pocket where I'd secured the ring, and lifted it out with shaking hands. I delivered the ring to Mary, setting it on top of her grave. I wasn't sure how, but the earth trembled and the ring disappeared into a small depression in the soil. Sam's ring—his fiancé's wedding ring, I realized—had finally been delivered.

When I recovered from the disappearance of the ring, I looked up to see the ghosts of Sam and Mary standing hand in hand. Sam's eyes were no longer wells of pain in a tortured face. His deep sorrow was transformed into pure joy. His entire face shone with happiness as he gazed wide-eyed and lovingly at Mary.

When the *Whydah* sunk, everyone thought that Mary was the one who cursed Sam Bellamy to die that day in a storm of her own making, but I could tell from how they looked at each other that that wasn't true. The true curse here was of a beautiful maiden and her handsome pirate love, cursed to spend eternity watching the waves, looking for their beloveds. And I had ended that curse. After three hundred years of waiting, Sam and Mary were finally together.

Tears streamed down my cheeks and I swallowed the lump forming in my throat. As Cal slipped his hand into mine, I glanced up to see him giving me the same look Sam was giving Mary.

"You did it, didn't you?" Cal asked, his voice soft.

While Cal squeezed my hand, I watched the glow of Sam and Mary's happiness grow until it was large enough to form a portal of light that they could both walk through side by side. Sam, still smiling, and Mary, wearing the ruby ring, waved at me and then disappeared.

The pirate crew was close behind. As The Grays entered the light, I saw their faces shift into expressions of delight, no longer tormented by the hardships of their mortal lives. Whatever bad deeds had earned these men their gray souls, they'd redeemed themselves in their devoted loyalty to their captain. They'd stuck with him until the very end.

I sniffed and let out a shaky breath, a smile growing on my lips.

"Yes," I said. "They're at peace now."

And I knew with every fiber of my being that it was true. Sam, Mary, and Sam's loyal crewmates had gone into the light and were finally at peace. Sam Bellamy's trip back to Mary Hallett had taken longer than expected—three hundred years longer—but the lovers had been reunited at last.

Chapter 27

The ride back to the beach house was quiet, each of us lost in our own thoughts. Even Simon was surprisingly silent as we left the Cape behind and Emma drove us north on I-95. I caught him casting mournful looks at Emma when he thought no one was looking. *Poor guy.*

Emma and Simon had become inseparable, but they would soon be parted by hundreds of miles. Emma was determined to go to veterinary school and focus on her medical training and Simon had sworn himself to Cal as pack lieutenant and was now bound by his duties to the pack. How many times would Simon have to ride down this highway on his motorcycle in the coming months, just to catch a glimpse of Emma between classes? Neither one of my friends would give up their own dreams and commitments, and for that I was thankful, but that meant they'd be spending a great deal of time apart in the next few years. I had a feeling that Emma's first semester of college would be tough on the both of them.

With thoughts of couples separated by distance, Sam and Mary and Simon and Emma, my eyelids began to droop. The turn of the wheels on asphalt lulled me to sleep and, for once, my dreams weren't interrupted by cryptic dung beetles or vengeful witches. The nightmare that had plagued me for months seemed to finally be gone for good. I didn't wake until Cal shook me gently and I raised my head from where it rested on his shoulder.

"Hey, sleepyhead," he said.

"Hey," I said, blinking rapidly. It was already after dark and Gordy had left the porch light on, waiting for our return.

"Sleep well?" he asked.

"Epic beauty sleep," I said.

"You don't need any more beauty," he said, tucking my hair behind one ear and sending shivers down my spine as his fingers brushed the sensitive skin. "You're already irresistible."

He leaned in and kissed the side of my mouth teasingly. I turned my head, slanting my lips to his. I gripped Cal's shirt in my hands, pulling him close. Cal thought I was the one who was irresistible? I needed him more than air.

We broke apart as London made a strangled sound and scrambled out of the car. I sighed and reached for the door. London obviously still had a thing for Cal. I needed to settle our duel before she got any more weird ideas into her head.

We made our way into the beach house where Gordy and Katie greeted us with platters of chili nachos for the guys, cheesy nachos for me, and jalapeno nachos for Emma. My stomach growled as Katie set the plate of cheese covered nachos in front of me and Gordy laughed.

"We missed you today," Katie said. "I'm glad you're back."

"You may not think so once I tell you what I have in mind for tonight," I said.

"More ghost stories around the bonfire?" she asked hopefully.

"Nope," I said. "An anime trivia face off, and I'm up first against London."

Katie sighed, but Gordy's eyes twinkled.

"This could be fun," he said.

"Glad you think so, because I need you to be our game show host for the first round," I said.

After eating my weight in nachos, which were delicious now that I wasn't being plagued by stinky ghost pirates, I went up to take a shower. When I came back downstairs, I found my friends and London waiting for me. Gordy had put on a button down shirt and funny old tie that probably belonged to one of his uncles.

"Let the anime trivia battles begin!" he said with lopsided grin.

London and I battled first and, as expected, she didn't stand a chance. I totally whooped London's butt with my anime knowledge, settling our duel. She sulked, of course, but I'd followed pack law to the letter and our duel had been witnessed by our pack alpha and first lieutenant. As much as she wanted, there was nothing she could do to change the verdict. I was the winner and she was the loser of this battle.

After our duel, we kept our distance. Cal had warned London that she was now on probation with the pack for threatening his mate behind his back, but she still flashed me the occasional glare. *Whatever.* I wasn't going to let one bully ruin my night.

I ignored London most of the time, focusing instead on a fun night of trivia battles with my friends. I was determined to enjoy every minute we all had left together while it lasted. The rest of the night was spent discovering how little most of my friends knew about anime. Simon, however, knew a surprising amount about the series Wolf's Rain. That boy has hidden talents.

Gordy and I had both been in our school's anime club together, so we took turns quizzing our friends and doing character impersonations. It was pretty hilarious. Later that night, when everyone else was getting ready for bed, Gordy showed me his newest drawings for the web comic he was working on. It was really good and featured a familiar looking redhead. There was chibi Katie cheering on her favorite surfer.

I laughed and went to bed feeling lighter than I had the day before. I'd returned Nera's amulet, helped the ghost pirates find their way into the light, spent a wonderful evening with my friends, and settled my duel with London. All in all, it had been a productive day.

The next morning, Cal made arrangements for London to stay with another werewolf family for a few days. Her family was on their way back from New York, but Cal didn't want London hanging around here for another day. His face darkened whenever anyone mentioned her name and I know he was thinking about the threats she'd made against me. But all of that was settled now and I was trying out a new personal goal of not living in the past.

I'd survived high school and the J-team's bullying, and had made it through London's attempts to steal Cal away from me. I'd even returned Nera's amulet to the Salem witches and, I think, made three new friends in the process. I was done with living in fear and picking at old scars. It was time to focus on the future.

The rest of the week was fun and relaxing as Gordy and Cal surfed and Katie, Emma, and Simon worked on their tans. I'd have to return to making preparations for the grand opening of my art stall, but this week was about spending time with my friends. And it's not like I wasn't working at all. I brought my paints and pencils to the beach each day, creating new pieces to add to my shop's inventory.

Once one morning, as I was staring at the sun rising on the ocean, I thought I saw the flicker of a large, wooden ship on the horizon. It sailed straight into the rising ball of flame and disappeared. I don't know if it was a trick of the light, but I could have sworn that I saw a flag sporting a skull and crossbones, the Jolly Roger, twitch from high atop the ship before it was swallowed into the sun.

I smiled, feeling another weight lift from my shoulders. I had a suspicion that Bellamy had been reunited with the *Whydah* crew. I looked around at my friends and felt my heart swell. We may spend time apart, due to college, or jobs, or other responsibilities, but we'd always be together in the ways that mattered—just like Mary, Sam, and his crew. When you have that kind of bond, nothing can keep you apart.

That night I slept better than I had in months, and since I was in my bed and not sitting in Emma's car there was no one to wake me prematurely. My dung beetle spirit guide was the only thing to enter my dreams, and even she only visited long enough to give me a brief message.

Life is short, little one, but love is forever.

I wasn't sure what I was supposed to do with that bit of knowledge, but I had already made a few early New Year's resolutions. Can you make New Year's resolutions in August? No matter what they were called, I'd made a list of new rules to live by. The first was to focus on the future, instead of the past. The second was to live life to the fullest. The third was to follow my dreams.

I was doing a pretty good job of sticking to my resolutions. They were much easier than the silly crash diets my mom tries in January. Maybe August was the best time for resolutions after all.

Chapter 28

One of my dreams was to pursue my art. Cal had helped make that dream a reality by putting a down payment on a rental space in downtown Wakefield, just a bike ride away from my parents' house. It had been his graduation present to me, a gift that kept on giving, just like Cal himself.

The rented space was a large stall off the local, indoor flea market where Cal and I often browsed for hours. But when I returned from the beach house, there was no time for shopping. There was still so much to do if the shop space was to be ready in time for my open house.

The next two weeks passed in a whirlwind of fabric and paint. Gordy and Katie posted flyers all over town, advertising the big night. Emma brought me tea, healthy snacks, and frequent pep talks and Simon took over some of Cal's workload with the pack so that my boyfriend could break away for much needed kisses...and to help me get the place ready. I think it was the kisses that helped keep me going, though don't tell Emma. She thinks it was her miracle tea.

Finally, it was the night of the open house and all of our hard work was paying off. The place looked fabulous and judging by the huge turnout my art gallery opening was a huge success. I'd rented the vacant stall across from my own, just for the night, and draped the walls in heavy, black fabric. Paintings and sketches hung from the walls, all except for one.

In the center of the makeshift gallery, where the aisle divided each stall, a large, heavy-framed painting sat on a wooden easel. The painting that took pride of place was of a handsome, young couple embracing in an old, overgrown Cape Cod cemetery. If the man looked like a notorious pirate and the girl resembled a certain legendary local witch, no one mentioned it. Everyone was too busy admiring the looks of love and adoration on the couple's faces to wonder who they were.

That was fine by me. It's not like I could explain how I'd managed to paint the actual Sam Bellamy and Mary Hallett, not without a trip to the funny farm and a brand new, tight fitting, white jacket. And I don't wear white, before or after Labor Day; it's just not my color.

It was getting late and as the night dragged on, I pretended to sip from my grape juice filled wine glass and eavesdropped on the last stragglers who were mingling in front of my paintings. I overheard their comments, of "mysterious," "fantastical," "abstract," and "figurative representation of the human condition" and tried not to giggle or snort unattractively into my glass.

Too bad most people's brains would explode if I told them the paintings of spirit auras were real. It would almost be worth their expressions of shock, but then again there was that whole white jacket thing. White was not the new black, no matter what the fashion gurus say.

My eavesdropping was interrupted as warm hands slid around my waist and Cal came to greet me from behind. He kissed the skin just below my ear and for a moment I forgot how to breathe.

"You look gorgeous," he said, his words whispering across my skin. He nipped at my neck and I nearly dropped my grape juice. *Pesky wolf.*

I was wearing a long, tight fitting, silk, off the shoulder dress—in black, of course—and I'd combed my hair into a deep part to fall in waves over my right shoulder. Emma said it was my knock-em-dead dress. I smoothed my hands down the front of the vintage dress, and smiled. I had to admit, I felt like a movie star in this get up. Thankfully, I had my leading man. Wolf. Whatever.

"Want to mingle?" I asked.

I'd had my share of rubbing shoulders with collectors and art enthusiasts, but wasn't sure how I was expected to end the evening—hence my suggestion to mingle. It had all seemed like a dream, and yet tonight had really happened. If the grand opening was any indication, I was the proprietor of a fairly successful art stall. Not too shabby for girl who smells dead people. I smiled despite my aching neck and shoulders.

"Not particularly, not with you in that dress," Cal said.

My breath caught as Cal's fingers began to glide up my side and over my shoulder. All thoughts of my aching neck and shoulders were gone in a flash. He reached up and cupped my face, turning me so that our eyes met, our lips bare inches apart.

"Mingling is highly overrated," I said, voice low.

If I had mastered the art of raising one eyebrow, I'd have done it. Instead, I licked my lips and considered our escape route. I'd need to return to close things up, but I probably wouldn't be missed if we slipped away for a moment.

Emma was doing a fabulous job as hostess and judging from the number of people leaving with wrapped canvases, Simon was charming the pants, um *wallets*, off our guests. Gordy and Katie were also helping with the catering. When I'd asked if I could hire them to serve mocktails and hors d'oeuvres, they'd jumped at the chance. Best. Friends. Ever.

I was seriously one of the luckiest girls on the planet, even with the seeing and smelling dead people. Speaking of luck, the hottest guy in the room was giving me a look of such adoration that I felt my heart swell to twice its usual size. Cal reached for my hand and I squeezed it in return.

With a grin tugging at my lips, I ducked under the black fabric that Cal held aside for me. Behind the curtain lay a cluttered storage area and a door to the loading docks. I followed him out the back of the building, across a two lane street, and up onto a hill that overlooked a small park.

The sun had set while I'd been inside and the area where we walked was dark, but a twinkling of light caught my eye. Down in the park, someone had decorated the trees, bushes, and lampposts with twinkling, white string lights.

I rubbed at my eyes, wondering if the lights were only ghosts playing a trick on me. But the message shining back at me was there when I lowered my hand. The lights spelled out the message, "I love you Yuki."

I blinked at the lights, then at Cal. He returned my startled look with a toothy grin, but his smile was soon replaced by a look of seriousness. Cal's eyes shone, reflecting the twinkling lights like a universe of stars, as he slid his hand into mine. His fingers twined with my own and his thumb stroked the sensitive skin at my wrist, sending delicious shivers up my spine.

"You are the most wonderful thing that has ever happened to me," he said.

Cal's eyes held mine as he lowered himself down onto one knee. I gasped as a wild herd of unicorns pounded inside my chest. *Was he...would he...?*

Cal reached up and took my other pale hand into his tanned one as his eyes searched my face.

"I want to be with you forever, Yuki," he said. "You are the only person I've ever loved, the only woman I ever wish to hold in my heart. You are my soul mate..."

His eyes filled with tears, but he didn't look away. I wanted to reach out and comfort him, to let him know that whatever it was, it would be alright. I bit my lip and squeezed his hands. Whatever he had to tell me, we would get through it together, like we always have, like we always will.

"Will you be my wife?" he asked.

I gasped, tears coming to my eyes to match the ones that were making Cal's eyes sparkle like sapphires. I knew what Cal was asking. He wasn't a normal man, with an average life. Marriage to him would mean making a commitment to his pack and an acceptance of who he really was.

Cal was a werewolf with ties to the moon that our bond could never break, no matter how much love there was in our hearts. He was both man and beast, and to love him, to marry him, would mean fully accepting the wolf as well as the man.

A feeling of weightlessness took over my body, leaving me breathless. Cal was asking if I would make that commitment, if I could accept all of the parts that made him whole. I licked my lips, trembling slightly as I gave my answer.

"Yes," I said. "Yes, of course I'll marry you Calvin Miller. All you had to do was ask."

Cal's arm twitched as our spirit tattoos flared in unison. My ankle tingled, a current of energy prickling the skin. The spirits of Cal's ancestors seemed to approve.

I lowered myself to my knees, Cal kissing me once before sinking to the grass, our bodies stretched out beneath the stars. As our lips met and Cal and I melted into each other, a low thrum vibrated from deep within the earth and a familiar voice filled my head.

"I have taught you all there is to know, child," my spirit guide whispered. *"Now it is up to you and your wolf. Find your happiness. Be the light that guides the spirits of the dead."*

I smiled against Cal's warm lips. Finding my happiness with Cal? I liked the sound of that.

Chapter 29

My spirit guide hadn't been entirely truthful; dang cryptic dung beetle. She hadn't truly taught me everything that I needed to know. There was still so much to learn if I was to be ready for this year's Samhain. Thankfully, I had the help of my new witch friends.

I received a lot of emails from the Salem witches during the final months before Halloween. Yes, they had email. They even sent text messages. At first I'd been surprised. I'd watched way too many scary movies and expected Evie, Gretchen, and Matilda to keep in touch by messenger bat or crystal ball. I sure had a lot to learn about witches.

With the help of my friends, I managed to make preparations for Samhain. I would have liked to have borrowed back Nera's amulet, but I couldn't risk that some new death speaker would need it more than me. So instead, I practiced mental focusing techniques with Simon, and learned protection magic from the witches. But the biggest surprise came from my parents.

Evie had mentioned that the death speaker gift ran in families, though the ability to sense the dead often skipped generations, happening only once or twice in a gifted family in a century. It was one of the reasons why people like me were so rare. But it meant that I probably hadn't been the only person in my family to sense the dead.

I'd often wondered if my paternal grandmother shared my gift. She'd died when I was young, but I'd been told that she suffered from terrible migraines—like the ones I got whenever I dealt with the deceased. And from what I'd been told, she was quite the eccentric. I always figured that was the polite word for crazy. But if I told people what I could see and smell, they'd think I was crazy too.

With so much to do, between the art stall and Samhain prep, I hadn't had a chance to ask my parents about my grandmother. My parents still worked long hours, which meant we rarely saw each other. So imagine my surprise when I got home late one night from work to see a light on in the kitchen.

I followed the light and smells of cooking food to find both of my parents sitting at the kitchen table. I'd caught them talking, but they went quiet when I entered the room. Not a good sign. I cleared my throat and went to the stove to see what they'd been making for dinner.

"You two are home early," I said. "And you cooked. What's the occasion?"

"Well, we thought it was time to share something with you, dear," Mom said.

She pushed something across the table and I realized it was a stack of old notebooks and journals. My father nodded at the books and tugged at his collar.

"We noticed a similarity between your paintings and some of the drawings in your grandmother's old journals," he said. "You never knew your grandmother, but she was a very…colorful person. We thought you might have an interest in reading more about her, now that you're grown up."

"Um, thanks," I said. I reached for one of the notebooks, but my mom brushed my hand away and scooped the books into a tote bag.

"You can read these later," she said. "We're getting ready to serve dinner. I made burritos and Spanish rice."

"Sounds great," I said.

I smiled and went to the sink to wash my hands. They weren't ready to talk about my gift yet, heck neither was I, but for the first time I wondered if my parents had known about my psychic abilities all along.

Later that week, when my parents were at work, Cal came over to help me read through the diaries. We were hoping for any clues as to how my gram survived the annual threat of Samhain, since once she reached adulthood the spirits of the dead would have been on her like zombies at a mathematics convention.

The books were spread across my comforter and Cal lay stretched out on the bed. I made sure my bedroom door was open before grabbing a journal and settling against the pillows. Ever since Cal's proposal, my parents insisted we keep the door open, even though they were hardly ever home. I thought the rule was silly, but stopped closing the door in order to keep my parents happy. It's not like I could claim that Cal and I were just friends while wearing an engagement ring.

My pulse raced as I caught sight of the sparkling ring on my finger. Cal had asked a jeweler to reset his grandmother's ring and I loved the idea of wearing a family heirloom. It made me feel even more connected to him. And now we were both reading through the notes my own grandmother had left behind.

Cal sucked in a breath and held a page up to me, eyes wide.

"Look at this," he said. "She started seeing ghosts when she was only sixteen."

"Here I was thinking that the seeing ghosts thing might have been jiggled loose early when I hit my head in the car accident," I said. "I had no idea I was such a late bloomer."

"And read what it says at the bottom of the page," he said, leaning closer.

After returning the amulet to the Salem coven, I despaired until learning of the effects of fennel. It was quite by accident that I discovered the reaction of evil spirits to this savory herb. Now I place it in all of my food, even going so far as to steep the herb and drink it as a tea, and place it in the pockets of my clothing. It does not deter my work with the kinder spirits, since to them it seems to have no effect whatsoever.

"This may be the answer we've been looking for," I said, eyes wide.

I jumped up, Cal close at my heels, and clomped down the stairs. At the kitchen, I dug through the spice cupboard until I found a bottle of fennel seeds wedged in with a crumpled recipe. I smoothed out the recipe card and laughed. Not only was fennel an easy to acquire herb, but, according to the recipe it was one that could be sprinkled on pizza. It was official. Pizza really was the answer to every problem.

Chapter 30

All too soon Samhain was here and I was confined in the Miller family cabin with Emma, Simon, and Cal. It was like old times, the four of us preparing to face down whatever supernatural baddies came our way.

Emma and Simon Skyped, texted, and emailed constantly, but this was Emma's first trip home since leaving for veterinary school at the beginning of September. The fact that they'd given up their first evening together to support me during the spirit storm made me feel all warm and fuzzy inside. Well, until they started arguing. That just set my teeth on edge.

"Don't even think about eating that tonight," Emma said, eyeing the package of ground beef in Simon's hand. She slid a scalpel out of her bag and twirled it while scowling at Simon. "Not unless you want to lose a finger."

"Come on, darling," he said. "Just one burger?"

"No," she said. "It's bad enough we'll be surrounded by the ghosts of dead people all night. We're not inviting the spirits of dead cows who suffered the horrors of the slaughterhouse."

"I'm sure their plight is quite moooving," he said.

I coughed, covering a chuckle, while Emma glared at Simon and waved the scalpel. Simon sighed and tossed the beef back in the fridge, rolling his eyes and holding up his hands.

"Fine, I won't eat any cows tonight, Love," he said. "Happy?"

"Extremely," she said.

Emma slipped the scalpel back into her vet kit and strode across the small kitchen and into Simon's arms. I looked away and focused on Cal. He was staring at me intently and I came to sit on the arm of his chair.

"What's up?" I asked. "Why so serious?"

"I'm worried about tonight," he said, flicking his eyes to the clock on the wall. It was nearly midnight. "Are you sure about this?"

"Yes, I'm sure," I said. "Gretchen said that if there are others like me out there, someone else might need the amulet tonight. Plus, I'm prepared." I pointed to my head. "This is well fortified thanks to Simon and his Jedi mind tricks. I did the cleansing ritual Matilda taught me, ate an entire pizza covered in fennel seeds, and I have my spirit army to defend me. What's to worry about?"

Actually, I *was* worried. As much as I wanted to believe in Matilda's spell and my grandmother's diaries, I had to admit that the witches spell was only supposed to dampen the effects of Samhain which meant relying on a crazy, old woman's journal. But I kept my chin high and smiled.

"I suppose you're right," he said. "I just can't stand the thought of something happening to you."

Cal reached up and pulled me into his lap. I could feel his muscles bunching beneath my hands as he wrapped his arms around me and buried his face in my hair. His lips slid to my ear as he whispered, "I love you. No matter what happens tonight. Remember that."

"I love you too," I said.

Cal's hand cupped my cheek and his lips slid to the edge of my mouth. I turned my face toward his, deepening the kiss. He tasted like sunshine, mint gum, and pine needles. A moment later the clock chimed midnight and the sunshine and pine needles were replaced by the smell of wet dog.

Cal tensed and pulled away to survey the room. Not that he could see anything. I, on the other hand, had my senses on overload. Matilda's protection spell helped to keep many of the smells at bay, but the scent of vinegar, burnt brownies, roses, rum, cooked meat, gun powder, salt brine, and apple blossoms filled the room.

Bright gold and dim gray ghost auras shot through the cabin walls and ceiling like the reflected light from a disco ball at a 70's dance party. I took a deep breath against a growing dizziness and focused on the front door. Seconds later, my ghost posse stepped inside.

Sam and Mary and The Grays, though I'd have to give them a new name since their auras were now shot through with gold, stood side by side with young Rose, the werewolf Garrett, and smelly Mr. Green. The spirits I'd helped throughout the past twelve months had come to me, every single one of them.

So much had changed since last Samhain. The past year hadn't always been easy, like the time the J-team had kidnapped me and threatened me with torture, but I was no longer afraid. I was surrounded by friends who loved me and spirits whom I'd helped into the light. They were all here to defend me and keep me safe. I grinned from ear to ear.

"Let's get this party started," I said.

Epilogue

*S*even years later I stood smoothing my long, red dress in front of a full length mirror as Emma and Katie fussed with my hair and makeup. My parents had asked that I wait until my twenty-fifth birthday to get married and Cal and I had agreed. We were in no hurry; our promise to each other was stronger than mere wedding vows. Our spirits were linked, a speaker of the dead and her wolf.

But now that the day had finally come around, I had to admit—I was excited. Okay, excited and terrified. I didn't like going up in front of groups of people and we'd opted for a big wedding. As head of the local werewolf pack, Cal had over five hundred pack members attending.

And that was just the people on his side of the aisle. I had my own motley fan club. Family members of the deceased filled the crepe paper covered seats.

Seven years can bring about a lot of changes and at some point I'd embraced my otherness and came out of paranormal closet. Of course, not everyone believed that I could see, and smell, the dead. Some skeptics even claimed it was a publicity stunt to sell more paintings. Not that I needed one. My artwork sold like body glitter at a vampire convention.

I loved my work helping spirits of the dead find their way into the light. I'd helped families find closure and even assisted the police on a few investigations. Along the way, my circle of friends had grown. But closest to my heart were my oldest friends, the ones who had believed in me and supported my dreams from the start.

I smiled and crossed my eyes as Emma tried to add another layer of white rice powder to my cheeks.

"Yuki," she muttered with a sigh. "Hold still."

"If you put any more of that stuff on me, my cheeks are going to be frozen solid," I said. "I'd like to be able to kiss the groom without my face cracking."

"It's your fault for wearing a red dress," she said. "Every time you blush, your deathly pale skin goes all blotchy."

"So what are you just standing there for?" I asked. "Add more powder, quick."

Katie giggled and went to grab my bouquet. Evie, Gretchen, and Matilda, my former nemeses, had picked out all of the bridal arrangements. My only request had been to include a sprig of apple blossoms to represent the most enduring love I'd ever witnessed, one that transcended even death. The rest I left up to my witch friends. Those three knew more about flower symbolism than I knew about manga.

Speaking of which, Katie had slipped around the corner to sneak a kiss from our favorite resident comic artist. Gordy accepted an internship with a renowned mangaka straight out of college and was now famous in his own right. His leading female characters were known for their trademark curly, red hair and perky personalities. I didn't have to wonder who his inspiration was; he was currently sucking face with her.

I smiled and Emma sighed.

"I give up," she said, tossing the makeup brush aside. "You're done."

"Can we see?" Katie asked.

"So long as by 'we' you mean you and Gordy," I said. "If Cal's hiding back there, he'll just have to wait. I'm not risking any more bad luck than I've already got."

Gordy and Katie rounded the corner hand in hand. When I turned around, they froze, mouths dropping open.

"Wow," Gordy said. "You look..."

"Gorgeous," Katie said.

"Um, thanks," said, trying not to blush. I didn't want Emma coming after me with more face powder.

"Are we ready?" my mom asked, squeezing into the already crowded room.

"I was born ready," I said, trying not to fidget.

"Oh, Yuki, you look beautiful," she said.

"Come on guys," Emma said. "Let's give these two a minute." Emma turned to me and winked. "You'll be fine. Just remember to breathe. We don't want you passing out when you're dad walks you down the aisle."

Great, now I was worrying about blushing *and* passing out. My mom shooed Emma and her medical advice out of the room. When everyone else was gone, she clasped her hand to her chest and smiled.

"I've waited so long for this day," she said.

"You've waited forever?" I asked. "I thought you and Dad wanted us to wait."

"You're father insisted you not rush into anything, but I've hoped you and Calvin would get married ever since you were kids," she said.

My mom always did love Cal. I smiled and gave her a hug.

"Thanks Mom," I said.

She squeezed me back then pulled away to wipe her eyes.

"I'll see you out there," she said, rushing out of the room. "You're father's right outside when you're ready."

I checked my reflection one more time in the mirror. My dark eye shadow and ruby, red dress wasn't traditional bride attire, but then again, I'd never been one for normal. I lifted the edge of my dress and checked the laces on my boots. No way was I risking wearing heels; I'd probably fall flat on my face.

I took a deep breath, smoothed the front of my dress, and stepped out to take my Dad's arm. At his nod, an organ started to play and all of our guests turned in their seats. My chest tightened as all eyes turned to face me. *You can do this Yuki.*

I searched for the one person who could always make me feel at ease. Cal stood at the front of the room. I'd recognized his broad shoulders and shaggy hair anywhere. As my eyes sought him out, the spirit tattoo on my ankle tingled and Cal turned to face me. I love seeing him in his usual faded jeans, but the tuxedo showed off his muscular body and trim waist to perfection. It was all I could do not to drool.

Cal flashed his high wattage smile, just for me, and my muscles loosened. I breathed deeply and found my feet able to match the tempo of the organ music, no longer worried about the crowd staring at me. They all faded away and it was just me and Cal. *I love you Calvin Miller.*

I took Cal's hand as I reached the altar and felt an inane grin spread across my face. I was grinning like a maniac, but I couldn't help it; I was crazy happy. I waited patiently through our vows until my favorite part.

"You may now kiss the bride," the justice of the peace said.

Before Cal could lean forward, I sprung up on tiptoe and kissed my husband. *Holy cannoli Batman.* Calvin Miller, the most powerful living werewolf, was now my husband. I could hear the whistles and cheers, and I'm pretty sure Simon hollered, "you show him, love," but I was lost in a sea of yummy Cal. When the heels of my boots started to retreat toward the floor, Cal lifted me into his arms and kissed me hungrily.

After we'd kissed fully, and probably messed up Emma's handiwork, Cal's lips slid from my mouth to whisper in my ear.

"I love you, Yuki," he said. "Now and forever."

Best. Wedding. Ever.

Acknowledgements

> Go on till you come to the end; then stop.
> --Lewis Carroll, *Alice's Adventures in Wonderland*

There are so many people who have helped to make this series possible. A huge thank you to my family and friends who tolerated endless distracted behavior and long absences. Heartfelt thanks to my best friend who helped to keep me sane through numerous rewrites and edits. To the many book bloggers out there who helped to spread the word about Yuki and the gang—you ROCK! Most of all, thank you for the support of readers like you.

Thank you all for joining me on this marvelous journey. I appreciate it more than you can ever know.

Coming in 2014
The first novel in the Hunters' Guild series
set in the world of Ivy Granger

E.J. Stevens

Hunting in Bruges

Read on for a sneak preview.

I've been seeing ghosts for as long as I can remember. Most ghosts are simply annoying; just clueless dead people who don't realize that they've died. The weakest of these manifest as flimsy apparitions, without the ability for speech or higher thought. They're like a recording of someone's life projected not onto a screen, but onto the place where they died. Most people can walk through one of these ghosts without so much as a goosebump.

Poltergeists are more powerful, but just as single-minded. These pesky spirits are like angry toddlers. They stomp around, shaking their proverbial chains, moaning and wailing about how something (the accident, their murder, or the murder they committed) was someone else's fault and how everyone must pay for their misfortune. Poltergeists are a nuisance; they're noisy and can throw around objects for short periods of time, but it's only the strong ones that are dangerous.

Thankfully, there aren't many ghosts out there strong enough to do more than knock a pen off your desk or cause a cold spot. From what I've discovered while training with the Hunters' Guild, ghosts get their power from two things—how long they've been haunting and strength of purpose. If someone as obsessed with killing as Jack the Ripper manifests beside you on a London street, I recommend you run. If someone as old and unhinged as Vlad the Impaler appears beside you in Târgoviște Romania, you better hope you have a Hunter at your side, or a guardian angel.

The dead get a bad rap, and for good reason, but some ghosts can be helpful. There was a woman with a kind face who used to appear when I was in foster care. Linda wasn't just a loop of psychic recording stuck on repeat; this ghost had free will and independent thought—and thankfully, she wasn't a sociopath consumed with bloodshed. Linda manifested in faded jeans and dark turtleneck and smelled like home, which was the other thing that was unusual about her. Most ghosts are tied to one spot, the place where they lived or died. But Linda's familiar face followed me from one foster home to another. And it was a good thing that she did. Linda the ghost saved my life more than once.

Foster care was an excellent training ground for self defense, which is probably why the Hunters' Guild uses it as a place for recruitment. Being cast adrift in the child welfare system gave me plenty of opportunities to hone my survival instincts. By the time the Hunters came along, I was a force to be reckoned with, or so I thought.

The Hunters' Guild provides exceptional training and I soon learned that attempts at both offense and defense were child's play when compared to our senior members. I didn't berate myself over that fact; I was only thirteen when the Hunters swooped in and welcomed me into their fold. But learning my limitations did make me painfully aware of one thing. If it hadn't been for Linda the ghost, I probably wouldn't have survived my childhood.

The worst case of honing of my survival skills had been at my last foster home, just before the Hunters' Guild intervened. I don't remember the house mother. She wasn't around much. She was just a small figure in a cheap, polyester fast food uniform with a stooped posture and downcast eyes. But I remember her husband Frank.

Frank was a bully who wore white, ketchup and mustard stained, wife-beater t-shirts. He had perpetual French fry breath and a nasty grin. It took me a few weeks to realize that Frank's grin was more of leer. I'd caught his gaze in the bathroom mirror when I was changing and his eyes said it all; Frank was a perv. Linda slammed the door in his face, but that didn't stop Frank. Frank would brush up against me in the kitchen and Linda would set the faucet spraying across the tiles...and slide a knife into my hand. My time in that house ended when Frank ended up in the hospital.

I'd been creeping back to the bedroom I shared with three other kids, when I saw Frank waiting for me in the shadows. I pulled the steak knife I kept hidden in the pocket of my robe, but I never got a chance to use it. Now that I know a thing or two about fighting with a blade, I'm aware that Frank probably would have won that fight. I tried to run toward the stairs, but Frank met me at the top landing. Frank reached for me while his bulk effectively blocked my escape. That was when Linda the ghost pushed him down the stairs. I remember him tumbling in slow motion, his eyes going wide and the leering grin sliding from his face.

Linda the ghost had once again saved me, but it seemed that this visit was her last. I don't know if she used up her quota of psychic power, or if she just felt like her job here was finally done. It wasn't until years later that I realized she was my mother.

I guess I should have realized sooner that I was related to the ghost who followed me around. We both have hair the same shade of shocking red. But where mine is straight and cropped into a short bob, Linda's was wavy and curled down around her shoulders. We also share a dimple in our left cheek and a propensity for protecting the weak and innocent from evil.

Linda the ghost disappeared, a wailing ambulance drove Frank to the hospital, police arrived at my foster house, and the Hunters swooped in and cleaned up the aftermath. It was from my first Guild master that I learned of my parents' fate and put two and two together about my ghostly protector.

As a kid I often wondered why Linda the ghost always wore a dark turtleneck; now I knew. Young, rogue vamps had torn out her neck and proceeded to rip my father to pieces like meat confetti. My parents were on vacation in Belize, celebrating their wedding anniversary when it happened. I'd been staying with a friend of my mother's, otherwise I'd be dead too.

I don't remember my parents, I'd only been three when I was put into the foster care system, but I do find some peace in knowing that doing my duty as a Hunter gives me the power to police and destroy rogue vamps like the ones who killed my mother and father. When I become exhausted by my work, I think of Linda's sad face and push myself to train harder. And when I find creeps who are abusive to women and children, I think of Frank.

That's how I ended up here, standing in a Brussels airport, trying to decipher the Dutch and French signs with eyes that were gritty from the twelve hour flight. It all started when my friend Ivy called to inform me that a fellow Hunter had hit our mutual friend Jinx. Ivy didn't know how that information would push all my buttons, she didn't know about Frank or my time in the foster system, but we both agreed that striking a girl was unacceptable. She was letting me, and the Hunters' Guild, deal with it, for now.

I went to master Janus, the head of the Harborsmouth Hunters' Guild, and reported Hans' transgressions. It didn't help that Hans had a reputation as a berserker in battle. The fact that he'd hit a human, the very people we were sworn to defend against the monsters, was the nail in the coffin of Hans' career.

I was assured that Hans would be shipped off to the equivalent of a desk job in Siberia. I should have left it at that, and let my superiors take care of the problem. But Jinx was my friend. Ivy's rockabilly business partner may have had bad luck and even worse taste in men, but that didn't mean she deserved to spend her life fending off the attacks of the Franks in the world.

Hans continued his Guild duties while the higher ups shuffled papers and prepared to send him away. Hans should have skipped our training sessions, but then again, he didn't know who had ratted him out—and the guy had a lot of rage to vent. I stormed onto the practice mat and saluted Hans with my sword. It wasn't long before the man started to bleed.

We were supposed to be using practice swords, but I'd accidentally grabbed the sharp blade I used on hunting runs. I didn't leave any lasting injuries, but the shallow cuts made a mess of his precious tattoos. I just hoped the scars were a constant reminder of what happens when you attack the innocent.

One week later, I received a plane ticket and orders to meet with one of our contacts in Belgium. I wasn't sure if this assignment was intended as a punishment or a promotion, but I was eager to prove myself to the Guild leadership. Master Janus' parting words whispered in my head, distracting me from the voice on the overhead intercom echoing throughout the cavernous airport.

"Do your duty, Jenna," he said. Master Janus placed a large, sword-calloused hand on my shoulder and looked me in the eye. I swallowed hard, but I managed to keep my hands from shaking. "Make us proud."

"I will, sir," I said.

"Good hunting."

E.J. Stevens is the author of the Spirit Guide young adult series and the bestselling Ivy Granger urban fantasy series. When E.J. isn't at her writing desk she enjoys dancing along seaside cliffs, singing in graveyards, and sleeping in faerie circles. E.J. currently resides in a magical forest on the coast of Maine where she finds daily inspiration for her writing.

CONNECT ONLINE

https://twitter.com/EJStevensAuthor
http://www.fromtheshadows.info
http://ivygrangerpsychicdetective.blogspot.com